Donut Library

1 SEPT 0?

24 JUN 12

GHOSTIFIED

SUPER SPOOKY

Massive thanks to my editor, Liz Bankes, who, I have a terrible feeling, wrote half this book. Thanks as ever to my brilliant agent Caroline Sheldon and to Jenny and Woody for listening to my stupid ideas.

First published in Great Britain in 2021
by Egmont Books UK Ltd
Text and illustrations copyright © Jim Smith 2021
ISBN 978 1 4502 9751 6
www.barryloser.com
www.egmontbooks.co.uk
70683/001

A CIP catalogue record for this title is available from the British Library

Printed and bound in Great Britain by the CPI Group

EGMONT
We bring stories to life

MIX
Paper from responsible sources
FSC® C020471

A SUPER WEIRD! MYSTERY ™

"Attack of the haunted lunchbox"

Jim Smith

Rhubarb & the gang

Hello and welcome to another amazing book all about Donut Island.

Donut is a completely round island with a giant hole in the middle of it.

Which is probably why it's called Donut Island.

This is Rhubarb Plonsky.

She's the editor of The Daily Donut, a school newspaper all about the super weird mysteries that happen here.

And this is Rhubarb's sidekick, Yoshi Fujikawa.

Yoshi's got a notepad which he's always scribbling stuff down in. ⟶

If you're listening to an audiobook, you'll just have to imagine what I'm saying, by the way.

This kid is Melvin Pebble.

He moved next door to Rhubarb in the last book.

At first, Melvin thought Rhubarb and Yoshi's mysteries were completely rubbish.

Then one day a massive slime monster climbed out of the giant hole and tried to eat everyone.

That changed his mind a bit.

Now Melvin works at The Daily Donut with Rhubarb and Yoshi.

Most of the time their mysteries are pretty rubbish, but every once in a while a good one comes along . . .

*Remember this object for later.

The O in Donut

It was a few minutes after I'd written chapter one and Rhubarb was sitting at home working on a new logo for The Daily Donut.

'What are you up to, Rubes?' asked her mum, Thelma, walking into the living room.

She obviously hadn't read the sentence before, had she?

'I'm working on a new logo for The Daily Donut,' said Rhubarb. 'It needs something with a little more pizazz!'

Thelma smiled. 'You really do love that newspaper, don't you?' she said, plonking her bum down on the sofa.

'The Daily Donut is my whole entire life,'
said Rhubarb, all seriously.

Thelma chuckled. 'My little detective!'
She stuck her hand down the side of
the sofa cushion and rummaged
around for the remote control.
'Haven't seen the remote,
have you?'

Rhubarb pointed across
the room. 'It's over there,'
she said, looking back down
at her sheet of paper.
'Argh, I can't get this
logo right!'

The
Daily
Donut

the
daily
donut

DD

Thelma leaned forwards and grabbed
something off the coffee table. It looked
like a red plastic arm with a yellow
rubber hand sticking out the end of it.

'This is a job for the

GRABBY GRABBER!'

she said.

The Grabby Grabber,
in case you didn't
know, is a handy
little gizmo that grabs
your remote control
when you can't reach
it. It was designed by
Rhubarb's dad, who
was a famous
inventor when he
was alive.

Thelma pressed a button on the side of
the Grabby Grabber and the rubber hand
sprung out, grabbing the remote control
and whipping it back to her.

'I dunno what I'd do without my trusty
Grabby Grabber.' Thelma smiled, turning
the TV on. 'There's no doubt about it,
your father was a very clever man.'

Rhubarb stared at the Grabby Grabber. 'Let me see that thing,' she said, grabbing it off her mum.

'That was his first big invention, you know,' said Thelma. 'Before the Grabby Grabber, people actually had to get up and walk over to their remote controls.'

Rhubarb smiled, thinking of her dad. She'd never known him, really. A crocodile ate him when she was just a baby.

'Grabby Grabber,' she said, reading the tiny words printed on the arm. And then she gasped.

'What is it, Rubes?' asked Thelma, as the theme tune to her favourite quiz show blurted out of the TV's speakers.

Rhubarb pointed at the writing on the Grabby Grabber. Underneath it in even tinier letters were the words, 'Made in Donut'. Except instead of a boring old normal 'o' in the word 'Donut', there was a drawing of a donut.

'That's exactly what my logo needs!' she said, scrunching her piece of paper up and grabbing a new sheet from the other side of the room with the Grabby Grabber.

Rhubarb sharpened her pencil and wrote 'The Daily Donut' on the new piece of paper, in her best bubble letters. Next she rubbed out a corner of the 'o' and drew three little curves to make it look like somebody had taken a chomp out of it.

She held the piece of paper up and smiled, just as the doorbell rang. 'Now that's what I call a logo!' she said, getting up and heading for the front door.

THE "SMELLY" "SIDE"

Rhubarb opened the front door, which is the sort of thing you do when a doorbell rings, isn't it.

Standing in front of her were Melvin and Yoshi.

'Guess what?' said Rhubarb, holding up her
sheet of paper. 'I've designed a new logo for
The Daily Donut!'

'That's brilliant!' said Yoshi. 'But even better,
I think we've got a new case.'

Rhubarb's nose drooped. She was a tiny bit
disappointed they weren't a tiny bit more
excited about her logo.

'Ooh, a new case,'
she said, folding
the paper up and
sniffing the air.
'It hasn't got
anything to do
with baked beans,
has it?'

Rhubarb can
sniff out a
mystery miles
away, in case
you didn't know.

Melvin gasped. 'That nose of yours is seriously impressive,' he said.

Yoshi whipped his notepad out of his pocket and flicked to the latest page. 'There's something super weird going on at Smelly Side Supermarket,' he said. 'The baked bean tins have been turning around by themselves.'

Rhubarb stroked her chin. 'Fascinating,' she said. 'Sounds like a job for the Daily Donut gang!'

The three of them zoomed across town, over to the other side of the giant hole in the middle of the island.

Melvin sniffed the air, copying the way Rhubarb had done it earlier. 'Poowee, it stinks over here!'

Rhubarb smiled at her friend. 'That's why it's called the Smelly Side,' she explained, as they strolled past a pongy cheese shop.

Yoshi looked around. 'I wish I lived here,' he said. 'It's where all the super weird stuff happens.'

They walked up to Smelly Side Supermarket and its glass doors swooshed open.

'This way,' said Rhubarb, heading straight for the tinned vegetables aisle.

Smelly Side Supermarket

Yoshi gasped. 'It's not just the baked beans that are round the wrong way,' he cried, pointing at the shelves. 'It's all of the tins!'

Rhubarb stared at the tins. Sure enough, every one had been twizzled so the back of its label faced outwards.

'This is bigger than we thought,' she said.

'It's awful,' agreed Melvin. 'How will customers know what they're buying?'

Rhubarb swivelled one of the tins round the right way.

'Yuck!' said Melvin. 'No wonder it's called the Smelly Side.'

Yoshi whipped his notepad out and jotted down what had happened so far. 'Let's see if any other products have been affected.'

The gang ran to the end of the aisle and hung a left. Melvin shrieked, pointing at a completely twizzled-round 24-pack of triple-ply toilet rolls.

Just then the manager, who was a frizzy haired woman, appeared from behind a display of man-size tissues. She was wearing a name tag with 'Gloria' written on it.

'Who are you lot?' she asked.

'We're from The Daily Donut,' said Rhubarb, handing her a business card. 'It seems you have a problem.'

'Yeah,' said Melvin, handing her his one too.

Rhubarb Plonsky
Editor, The Daily Donut

All Mysteries Investigat

Melvin Pebble
Associate Investigator,
The Daily Donut

All Mysteries Investigat

Gloria pincered the cards and gave them a quick read. 'It's happening on the fruit aisle too,' she said.

They all ran towards the fruit aisle and skidded to a stop in front of a giant pyramid of satsumas.

'Hang on a second, how do you know if these have been twizzled?' asked Rhubarb. 'They don't have any labels.'

'Yeah, just these little barcodes,' said Melvin, pointing at a tiny round sticker on one of the satsuma's bums.

Gloria picked a satsuma up and the whole entire pyramid collapsed. 'You don't work at Smelly Side Supermarket for thirty-seven years without knowing a thing or two about tangerines,' she said.

'Erm, the sign says satsumas,' said Yoshi, but Gloria just shrugged.

'Tangerines, satsumas, what's the difference?' she said, as one of them rolled towards Rhubarb and bumped against her shoe.

Rhubarb picked the satsuma up and sniffed it.
Then her eyes opened wide.

'What is it, Rubes?' asked Melvin, but she didn't
answer. She was too busy staring at a man
holding what looked like a Grabby Grabber.

The Phantom Twizzler

'What's he up to?' said Gloria, peering at the man. He was wearing a black and white stripey anorak and looked kind of like a giant, person-shaped version of a barcode.

He pressed the button on the side of his Grabby Grabber and the yellow rubber hand sprung out and picked up a sprig of broccoli.

'Hey, he's twizzling that broccoli!' cried Rhubarb, zooming over and tapping him on the shoulder.

31

The man turned round, still holding the broccoli in his Grabby Grabber. 'May I help you, young lady?' he asked. In his other hand, he was carrying one of those barcode zapper thingys you can get.

'We were just wondering what you were doing,' said Rhubarb to the man.

'I'm beeping barcodes,' he said, zapping
the little barcode sticker on the broccoli.
Something did a buzz inside his pocket.

He stuck his hand into it and whipped a
phone out, then slid his finger across the
screen. A million barcodes popped up and he
scrolled though them, proudly. 'I'm collecting
every one in the whole of Donut!'

'Yeah, and twizzling my tins round while
you're at it,' said Gloria.

Rhubarb stroked her chin. 'The Annoying Case Of The Phantom Barcode Twizzler,' she said. 'Write that down, Yoshi. I think we'll put it on the front page.'

'The Phantom Twizzler, eh?' said the man. 'I like the sound of that!'

Yoshi looked up from his notepad. 'Can I take your real name, too?' he asked. 'It's for The Daily Donut.'

'David Splurg,' said the man, and Melvin sniggled.

Gloria pointed to the doors. 'Yeah well, you're banned from Smelly Side Supermarket, David Splurg!' she boomed.

'Alright, alright, keep your hair on,' said David Splurg, trudging off towards the exit. 'But this isn't the last you've heard of the Phantom Twizzler!'

Rhubarb put her arms round Melvin and Yoshi. 'Another mystery solved,' she said.

'Thanks for your help, kiddos,' said Gloria, heading off to the tinned vegetables aisle to do some de-twizzling.

Melvin stroked his chin, copying the way Rhubarb had just done it. 'We're getting pretty good at this detective business, aren't we?' he said.

Rhubarb smiled, happy he was enjoying being part of The Daily Donut. 'We certainly are, Melv,' she said, as the three of them started walking home.

Cheese & pickle sarnie

It was the next morning and Rhubarb was in her kitchen, making her packed lunch. She'd stayed up late the night before, writing up Yoshi's notes for The Annoying Case Of The Phantom Barcode Twizzler.

'Morning, Rubes,' said Thelma Plonsky, trudging into the room. She waved her hand in front of one of the cupboard doors and it swished upwards, disappearing into a slot in the ceiling.

She grabbed her favourite green mug and walked over to the sink, pressing a big brown button next to it. Steaming hot coffee poured out of the tap, straight into the mug.

I stole this from Donut Diner.™

Next she pressed a white button, and ice cold milk started to dribble out of the tap. 'That's enough, thank you, Tappy,' she said, and the milk stopped dribbling. 'I've said it before and I'll say it again. That dad of yours was a very clever man, Rhubarb.'

Rhubarb smiled as she sliced a cheese and pickle sandwich in half. She plonked it on the counter next to a carton of apple juice, a packet of salt and vinegar crisps, a chocolate bar and a satsuma.

Or maybe it was a tangerine.

She glanced around for her lunchbox, which was usually lying on the draining board, all washed up and ready for another day at school. 'That's funny, I can't find my lunchbox.'

'Oops, sorry Rubes,' said Thelma. 'I put the leftover bolognese in it last night.' She bent down and stuck her head into a cupboard then stood back up, placing a metal box on the counter.

'What's that?' asked Rhubarb. She'd never spotted it before.

'It's your Dad's old lunchbox,' said her mum.

* Remember?

The lunchbox was blue and had lots of different-shaped panels on the sides. Next to each panel was a little red button.

'Check this out,' said Thelma, pressing one of the buttons. A triangle-shaped panel slid open to reveal a small compartment behind it. A metal arm with a claw on the end shot out and grabbed the cheese and pickle sandwich.

SNATCH!

'Wow, is it one of Dad's inventions?' asked Rhubarb, as the claw disappeared back into the lunchbox, along with the sarnie.

Thelma nodded. 'Terry never went anywhere without his Self-Packing Lunchbox,' she said.

'What, even to the toilet?' asked Rhubarb, pressing four more buttons. Four of the panels slid open and four metal arms reached out and grabbed the carton of apple juice, the packet of salt and vinegar crisps, the chocolate bar and the satsuma.

'Well no, not the toilet,' said her mum.

'What about to bed?' asked Rhubarb. 'Are you telling me he took his Self-Packing Lunchbox to bed?'

Her mum rolled her eyes. 'Alright, so maybe he didn't take it everywhere,' she said. 'I just meant he loved his Self-Packing Lunchbox, that's all.'

Rhubarb stuffed it into her rucksack. 'Well if my dad made it, then I love it too,' she said, kissing her mum on the cheek and heading for the door.

The Newshound Award

Rhubarb opened the front door to see Melvin standing there with his finger pointing out, just about to ring the bell.

'You can ring it if you want,' said Rhubarb, feeling a bit sorry for him, missing out on a nice doorbell ring like that.

'Nah, it's OK,' said Melvin, as they started strolling down the street. 'There's always another doorbell.'

'Where's Yoshi?' asked Rhubarb.

'Right here,' said Yoshi, strolling up behind them.

They turned left on to Donut High Street
and Melvin looked down at his trainers. 'Hey,
what's with the pavement today?' he said.
'It feels all squidgy.'

Rhubarb took a couple of steps forward.
'You're right, it is a bit on the squidgy side.
Well spotted, Melv.'

'The Mysterious Case Of The Squidgy Pavement,' said Yoshi, scribbling it down in his notepad. 'What do you reckon, Rubes?'

'I like it,' said Rhubarb, as they walked through the gates of their school.

You know that bit when you're walking from the gates of your school towards your classroom? I completely can't be bothered to write about it.

'Morning, kiddos!' said their teacher, Mr Thursday, once everyone had squidged their bums into chairs. 'I've got some very exciting news for three of you today.'

He looked at Rhubarb, Yoshi and Melvin, who were sitting in the front row. 'Ooh, spill the baked beans, Mr Thurs!' said Rhubarb.

Hector Frisbee, who was slumped in the back row, laughed. 'Keep it cool, Plonsky,' he said.

Hector is the leader of The Cool Doods, in case you didn't know.

'Yeah Plonsky,' said his sidekick, Marjorie Pinecone. 'Keep it cool.'

'Yeah, keep it cool, Plonsky,' said Dirk, who's Hector's other sidekick.

The Cool Doods are idiots, by the way.

Mr Thursday ignored The Cool Doods and smiled at Rhubarb. 'I've entered The Daily Donut into the Newshound Award,' he said.

'The Newshound Award?' said Yoshi. 'How exciting!'

'I can't believe we've been entered into the Newshound Award!' said Melvin.

'What's the Newshound Award?' asked Rhubarb.

Melvin looked at Rhubarb. 'Yeah that's a point, what's the Newshound Award?'

Mr Thursday chuckled. 'It's a competition to find the best newspaper story in the whole of Donut Island,' he said.

'Do you really think we could win?' asked Rhubarb.

'Absolutely,' said Mr Thursday. 'It'd have to be a real story, though. Not like that slime monster one you came up with. Although I have to say, it really was a cracker!'

Melvin blinked. 'But we didn't make that up, Mr T. It really did happen.'

Rhubarb nudged her next-door neighbour. 'Don't be silly, Melv, of course we made it up,' she said.

That was the thing about the mystery of the

that tried to eat everyone on Donut Island.
Nobody apart from Rhubarb, Melvin and
Yoshi remembered it actually happening.

Melvin winked at Rhubarb. 'Ohhh yeahhh,
of course we made it up,' he said.

'Anyway,' said Mr Thursday. 'The deadline's
tomorrow night. Sorry for the short notice,
I only just heard about it myself.'

'No problemo,' said Rhubarb. 'The Daily Donut
gang are on the case!'

Hector Frisbee put his hand up, but only halfway, because putting it all the way up wouldn't've looked very cool. 'Can anybody enter?' he asked.

Mr Thursday thought for a second. 'I suppose. But you've got to have a newspaper.'

'What if we started one right now?' asked Hector.

Rhubarb rolled her eyes. 'Since when are you interested in newspapers?'

Hector smiled. 'Since it started annoying you.'

Marjorie chuckled. 'We could call it The Daily Cool Doods,' she said.

53

'The Daily Cool Doods?' said Rhubarb, quickly counting up how many donuts you could fit into its logo.

The Daily

'That's the stupidest name I ever heard.'

'Yeah, that name is SO stupid,' said Melvin. 'Plus what would you even write about, anyway?'

'Cool stuff that happens on Donut Island?' said Dirk. 'Like when Hector says something cool, we could just write it down and put a photo of him next to it.'

Hector high-fived Dirk.
'Nice idea, Measles.'

'Thanks, boss,'
said Dirk.

Mr Thursday
shrugged. 'Well,
there's nothing
to stop you having
a go if you fancy it.'

'That's that, then,' said Hector,
pushing his sunglasses up his nose.
'May the coolest paper win.'

Rhubarb scoffed. 'Good luck, Frisbee,'
she said. 'Because you're gonna need it.
Because your paper is going to be rubbish.
And The Daily Donut is completely going
to win. End of story.'

Except it wasn't the end of the story.
It was just the end of this chapter.

Brenda the hut

After a trillion hours of really boring lessons it was first break.

'Last person to Daily Donut HQ smells like a twizzled-round tin of luxury fermented miniature cabbages in vinegar!' said Rhubarb, running across the playground and jumping over a fence into a tiny forest.

Hidden amongst the trees sat a little shed. 'In memory of Brenda the dinner lady,' it said on a plaque above the door.

'Ah, don't you just love Brenda the Hut,' said Yoshi, as they stepped inside.

Brenda the Hut's windows were as filthy as the glass in real life Brenda's glasses. A set of shelves were screwed into one wall, a collection of strange items lined up on them.

There was a jam jar filled with green slime, a little plastic ball lying at the bottom of it. This was a Donut Hole Monster, which you'd know all about if you'd read the book before this one.

Next to that were some other things which I can't be bothered to describe.

'Right, what are we going to write about for this Newshound Award?' said Rhubarb. 'We can't let The Daily Cool Doods win!'

Rhubarb lifted her dad's old lunchbox out of her ruck sack and plonked it on the table.

Melvin stared at it. 'Cool lunchbox,' he said.

* Fed up with this drawing yet?

'Thanks, Melv,' said Rhubarb. 'It was my dad's. He was carrying it when he got eaten by the crocodile.'

Melvin's eyeballs popped out of their sockets and rolled across the floor, fell out the door and landed in a puddle.

Not really.

'Hang on a millisecond,' he said. 'Your dad was eaten by a crocodile?'

Rhubarb nodded. 'I mean, I think he was carrying it when the crocodile ate him. My mum says he never went anywhere without his Self-Packing Lunchbox.'

'Whoa, whoa, whoa,' said Melvin. 'Your DAD was EATEN by a CROCODILE?'

Rhubarb nodded again. 'Yeah, when I was a little baby. You didn't know?'

Melvin shook his head. 'No, Rhubarb, I didn't know your dad was eaten by a crocodile when you were a baby. What exactly happened?'

'He was in Donut Zoo and a crocodile ate him,' said Rhubarb. 'Nobody knows anything else. Now, how about some ideas for the Newshound Award?'

Melvin went quiet for a second, taking in the fact that a crocodile had eaten his next-door neighbour's dad. 'Erm, well how about the Phantom Twizzler?' he said.

'Hmm, I dunno if it's got enough pizazz,' said Rhubarb.

Yoshi flicked through his notepad.
'Squishy pavements?' he said.

The
Mysterious
Case Of
The
Squishy
Pavement

OMG
we've been
entered into
The
Newshound
Award!
(what even
is it?)

'Perfect!' said Rhubarb, her tummy doing
a rumble.

'Somebody needs a mid-morning snack,'
said Melvin, sounding like a bit of an old
granny.

'Good idea,' said Rhubarb, looking at all
the buttons on her lunchbox. 'Now, which
compartment did my chocolate bar
disappear into?'

She spotted a rectangle-shaped panel about the size of a chocolate bar and pressed the red button next to it.

'Cool!' said Melvin, as the panel slid open.

And then he started screaming.

Terry Plonsky

The reason Melvin was screaming was that a chubby, see-through man had stuck his head through the slot of the lunchbox.

'Ooh, my back!' said the man, squeezing the rest of his body out and floating into the air. 'Boy, am I glad to get out of there.'

'IT'S A GHOST!' cried Melvin.

Yoshi dropped his notepad. 'H-how did you fit inside that lunchbox?'

'IT'S A GHOST!' cried Melvin, again.

Rhubarb took a step forward. 'D-dad?' she whispered, staring up at the ghost.

Yoshi and Melvin gasped.

The see-through man peered down at Rhubarb. 'Rubes?' he said. 'Can that really be my little girl?'

A tiny little firework exploded inside Rhubarb's stomach. 'Yes, it's me,' she said. 'And you're ...'

'A GHOST!' cried Melvin, again.

Her dad looked down at himself. 'Yeah, funny that, isn't it,' he said.

They all stood there for a second, except for Rhubarb's dad, who was floating.

'Come here Rubes,' he said, wrapping his arms around Rhubarb. It felt weird, sort of like being hugged by a cloud.

A tear ran down her cheek, but not a sad one. 'Melvin, Yoshi, this is my dad, Terry Plonsky.'

Yoshi did a little wave. 'Er, nice to meet you, Mr Plonsky.'

'YOU'RE A GHOST!'

cried Melvin.

Terry chuckled. 'Hello, fellas,' he said, looking at his daughter. 'Crikey, you've grown up, Rubes. How's your lovely mum?'

'She's good,' said Rhubarb. 'Misses you, of course. We both do. I mean, did. Blimey, this is weird!'

Yoshi tapped Terry on the shoulder, his finger half disappearing into it. 'I hope you don't mind me asking, but what does it feel like being eaten by a crocodile?'

Terry scrunched his face up. 'No idea,' he said. 'Why do you ask?'

Rhubarb blinked. 'You mean you don't remember?'

'Don't remember what?' said Terry.

'It's a long story,' said Rhubarb, even though it actually wasn't.

See-through snacks

'But how did I end up inside that thing?' asked Terry, once Rhubarb had told him everything.

Rhubarb stared at the Self-Packing Lunchbox. The rectangle-shaped panel her dad floated out of had shut again, but something was stuck in it. 'Hey, what's that?' she said, giving it a tug.

'Looks like a sticky note,' said Yoshi. 'Except completely see-through.'

Rhubarb held the transparent scrap of paper up. 'Meet me down Donut Zoo,' she said, reading what was scrawled on it.

'It's signed,' said Melvin, pointing at the bottom corner, which was torn. Sure enough, somebody had written their name on it. The only problem was, everything except the first letter had been ripped off.

'T,' said Rhubarb, reading out all that was left of the signature. 'Maybe it's for 'Terry'?'

'Why would your dad be carrying a note around telling him to meet himself down Donut Zoo?' said Yoshi.

Rhubarb thought for a second. 'You're right,' she said. 'It looks like somebody wanted him to go there.'

Yoshi scribbled that in his notepad. 'But who? And how did he end up inside that lunchbox?'

Terry scratched his bald, see-through head. 'It's a mystery, all right.'

'That's it!' said Melvin. 'That's the mystery we'll write about for the Newshound Award.'

Rhubarb didn't say anything, which was kind of weird for her, especially when it came to mysteries.

'What's the matter, Rubes?' asked Terry.

Rhubarb looked at her dad. 'There's something weird about this one.'

'I thought weird was good?' said Melvin.

'Yeah, it is,' said Rhubarb. 'Forget I mentioned it.' She nudged her dad. 'Now, we have to jog your memory somehow.'

Suddenly her tummy did another rumble. Rhubarb pressed the button next to another rectangle-shaped slot, and this time her chocolate bar plopped out. Except it wasn't an ordinary chocolate bar any more. It was see-through and hovering.

'Twizzling tangerines,' cried Melvin. 'It's turned into a ghost as well!'

Yoshi pushed his glasses up his nose. 'It's been GHOSTIFIED,' he said.

'Ghostified?' said Rhubarb. 'What's that?'

73

Yoshi reached up to the shelf and grabbed a small book. 'It's something I read in here,' he said, flicking through it.

Rhubarb pressed four more buttons on the lunchbox. Four slots slid open and a see-through cheese and pickle sandwich, carton of apple juice, packet of salt and vinegar crisps and satsuma floated out.

'Hey look, they've all been ghostified too!'
said Melvin, trying to snatch the packet of
crisps, but his hand went straight through it.

'Cute little guys, aren't they,' said Terry,
grabbing the sarnie and taking a bite. He
looked at his old metal lunchbox. 'What's
the deal with that thing, anyway?'

Rhubarb picked it up. 'It's a Self-Packing Lunchbox. You invented it, remember?'

Terry looked surprised. 'I'm an inventor?'

'The greatest inventor in the whole of Donut Island,' said Rhubarb.

Her dad blinked. 'Blimey. What else did I invent?'

Rhubarb smiled. 'You'll have to read the next chapter to find out!'

Unfinished business

Rhubarb didn't really say that last bit, by the way.

What she actually said was, 'You invented the SUCK & BRUSH!'

Terry looked at his daughter like he didn't know what she was talking about.

'Your dad invented the SUCK & BRUSH?' cried Melvin. 'I've always wanted one of those!'

Terry smiled, even though he still didn't know what anyone was talking about. 'What does it do?'

Rhubarb whipped her phone out of her pocket, opened up the Donut Tube app and typed, 'SUCK & BRUSH advert' into the search bar.

The screen went fuzzy then a kid appeared, holding a strange looking toothbrush. 'I used to HATE brushing my teeth,' said the kid. 'Then my mum bought me a SUCK & BRUSH!'

78

The kid squeezed a blob of toothpaste on to the brush then pressed a button on the handle. The SUCK & BRUSH started to whir, and fizzy brown liquid squirted out of the bristles.

'Now I LOVE brushing my teeth!' said the kid, slurping on cola while polishing his gnashers.

The SUCK & BRUSH logo popped up on the screen. 'May cause really bad cavities, teeth will probably fall out after continued use,' whispered a sped-up voice over the top of it.

Terry frowned. 'Doesn't sound very good for your chompers,' he said.

'That's why my mum won't buy me one,' said Melvin.

Yoshi chuckled. 'Tell us something else you invented, Mr P.'

'Ask her,' said Terry, pointing at his daughter.

Rhubarb thought for a second.

'Ooh, there's so many,' she said. 'EAR BUGS, FINGER LIDS . . .'

'FINGER LIDS,' said Yoshi, like the words rang a bell. 'Doesn't your mum have a set of those?'

Rhubarb nodded. 'Yeah, she loves them,' she said.

'They're those little lids you put on the ends of your fingers, aren't they?' said Melvin.

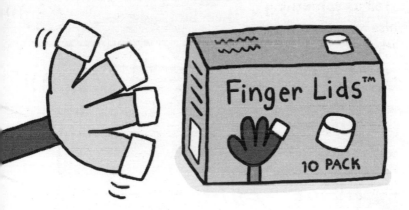

Terry scrunched his face up. 'Why would you ever put lids on the ends of your fingers?' he said.

'To keep them nice and clean when you're not using them,' said Rhubarb.

'When is anyone not using their fingers?' said Terry, scratching his bum, and right there on the spot he disappeared, along with Rhubarb's floating snacks.

'Hey, where'd you go?' said Rhubarb.

'I'm right here,' said Terry's voice.

Yoshi pointed at a page in his ghost book.

'It's a well known fact that ghosts disappear when they scratch their bums,' he said.

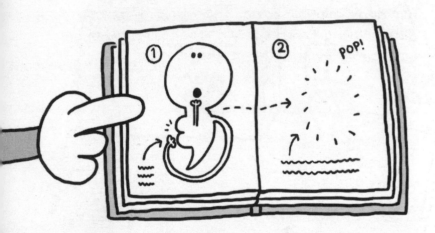

Melvin sniggled. 'You learn something new every day,' he said, sounding like a bit of old granny for the second time that morning. 'What else does it say in this book of yours?'

Yoshi peered down at the page. 'Nobody knows why ghosts exist,' he said, reading out a sentence. 'Some believe they are here to complete unfinished business.'

'Unfinished business?' said Terry's voice, grabbing the book. 'Let me have a look at that.'

Just then, the bell started to ring. 'Come on, let's get back to class,' said Melvin.

Rhubarb glanced over at THE LITTLE BOOK OF GHOSTLY FACTS, which was floating in her dad's invisible hand. The whole thing was disappearing from the bottom up, and she guessed he must be slotting it into his pocket.

'Maybe you lot should go ahead without me,' he said. 'I'm a bit old for school.'

'Don't be silly,' said Rhubarb, grabbing the Self-Packing Lunchbox and heading back to class. 'Just don't go scratching your bum!'

Donut
High
Street

Donut Island Council

Rhubarb's dad stayed invisible for the rest of the day, but he made sure she knew he was there.

Like in Science, when he tapped Hector Frisbee on the shoulder. Fifteen times. Every fifteen seconds.

For the whole lesson.

TAP TAP!

And at lunch when he picked up Marjorie Pinecone's banana, peeled the skin and took a giant bite.

'Waaah, it's the ghost of Brenda the dinner lady!' screamed Marjorie, running out of the canteen with her arms waggling.

'You crack me up, Mr Plonsky,' said Yoshi, as the Daily Donut gang strolled through the gates after school.

Rhubarb smiled. It was nice to have a real life dad at last, even if he was a ghost.

'All part of the service, Yoshi baby,' said Terry, scratching his bum and reappearing.

Rhubarb yelped. 'What are you doing?' she
said, reaching over and scratching his bum
herself, and he disappeared again.

'What do you mean, what am I doing?'
said Terry, re-scratching his bum and
re-reappearing.

'You can't scratch
your bum!' said
Rhubarb, scratching
his bum again, and
he re-disappeared.

SCRITCH
SCRATCH!

Terry scratched
his bum for the
third time in
three seconds.
'Why not?' he
said, re-reappearing
again.

'Because we can't
let anyone see
you!' whispered Rhubarb, giving
her dad's bum one last scratch.

'Oh yeah, sorry Rubes,' he said,
disappearing in a puff of blow-off.

Just then, Mr Thursday strolled up behind them. 'What was that?' he asked.

'What was what?' said Rhubarb, hiding her hand behind her back.

'I could've sworn I saw a chubby see-through man floating in the air,' said Mr Thursday.

Rhubarb did a little chuckle. 'You've been working too hard, Mr Thursday,' she said. 'Lucky it's the weekend tomorrow, you should put your feet up and relax.'

Melvin nodded. 'Sounds like you've been reading too many Daily Donut stories,' he said, winking at Rhubarb.

'Yeah Mr Thursday,' said Yoshi. 'As if Rhubarb's dad has come back to life as a ghost and the only way to make him disappear is to scratch his bum!'

'Ha, ha, yes well,' said Mr Thursday, giving Yoshi a funny look, and he headed off down the road. 'Good luck with the Newshound Award!'

They turned on to Donut High Street and Rhubarb spotted The Cool Doods, standing outside Donut Pizza.

'Shhh,' whispered Hector, as the Daily Donut gang strolled up. 'Here they come now.'

Rhubarb sniffed the air, but couldn't smell anything. 'What's going on here?' she asked.

Dirk pulled a notepad, just like Yoshi's, out of his pocket and scribbled something in it. 'Wouldn't you like to know,' he said.

'Yeah, it's top secret,' said Marjorie.

Rhubarb stared at Hector. Something was sticking out of his left earhole. But from the way he was standing, she couldn't quite see it.

'Come on, tell us!' she said, waggling her nostrils. If there was one thing she hated, it was a mystery she couldn't smell.

'Just you wait and see,' said Hector. 'You won't believe your eyes. Or should I say, EARS!'

He turned around, cackling, and strolled into Donut Pizza with Dirk and Marjorie following.

The Daily Donut gang crossed the road. 'So I was thinking, how about a trip to Donut Zoo?' said Rhubarb. 'Seeing as that's where dad got eaten and everything.'

'Thanks for the reminder,' said Terry.

Melvin looked down at his trainers. 'Hey look,' he said. 'The pavement's still all squishy.'

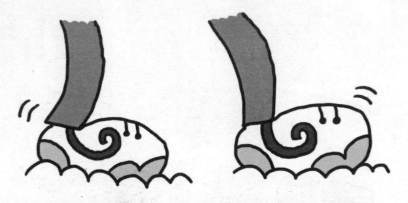

'Super Weird,' said Rhubarb. 'But there's no time for that. The Cool Doods are already working on their story and we haven't even started!'

Terry stroked his chin, not that anyone could see him doing it. 'Those trainers of yours,' he said to Melvin. 'They remind me of something.'

Rhubarb stopped walking and twizzled round on the spot. 'What is it, Dad?' she asked. 'It could be important.'

'I'm not sure,' said Terry. 'Maybe it's one of my inventions?'

They all stood there for a second, trying to work out what it was. 'I've got it,' said Rhubarb.

"TRAINER TRAINERS!"

TRAINER TRAINERS™

Rhubarb typed the words 'TRAINER TRAINERS' into her phone and held the screen up to her dad's face, or where she thought it was, anyway.

'TRAINER TRAINERS,' boomed a voice, as a girl wearing a pair of bright white trainers slipped her feet into a much bigger, even brighter pair.

'BECAUSE WALKING IS BORRRRR-RING!'
boomed the voice again.

Five small metal legs with tiny white
trainers on the ends of them popped
out of the soles of the TRAINER TRAINERS
and started to stroll.

'TRAINER TRAINERS,' boomed the boomy
voice. 'TRAINERS FOR YOUR TRAINERS.'

'Trainers for your trainers?' said Terry.
'Is it just me, or were all my inventions
completely ridiculous?'

'TRAINERS TRAINERS are the coolest!' said Melvin. 'My mum won't buy me those either.'

'I think Hector's got a pair,' said Yoshi.

Melvin sighed. 'I wish I had Hector's mum.'

Rhubarb stuffed her phone back in her pocket. 'Well at least your memory's coming back a bit,' she said to her dad. 'Now let's get down Donut Zoo.'

They started walking again, past a shop called Donut Pottery.

'COME IN AND MAKE A TEACUP OR SOMETHING,' said the words on a giant poster in the window.

'Ooh, can we go in there?' said Terry.

Rhubarb did the face she does when she doesn't want to go into a pottery shop.

'I thought we were trying to work out how you ended up inside your lunchbox?' she said.

'I know,' said Terry. 'But we never got to do stuff like this when you were little. Plus I've always fancied making a teacup.'

Rhubarb stroked her chin. On one hand, all she wanted to do was get down Donut Zoo and sniff out some clues. But on the other, her dad was right. They'd missed out on so much stuff, and this was their chance to catch up.

All of a sudden a crocodile appeared from behind a rubbish bin and chomped Rhubarb's hand off. Not in real life though, just inside her head.

'Oh, go on then,' she said, opening the door to Donut Pottery.

Mrs Terrible

They walked into the shop and a grumpy looking lady glared at them from the back of the room. A name tag on her jumper said 'Mrs Terrible'.

'Funny old name for a pottery shop owner,' whispered Terry, who obviously had very good eyesight for a middle-aged ghost.

'What do you lot want?' grumbled the lady.

'We were wondering if we could make
a teacup or something,' said Rhubarb.
'We're in a bit of a hurry, though.'

Mrs Terrible grabbed three lumps of
clay and flomped them on to
a table.

The kids sat down and Rhubarb ripped
her lump in half, passing one bit to her
invisible dad.

'Just keep the noise down,' snapped Mrs
Terrible, stomping back to her own table.
'I've got some very important work to do.'

Terry started rolling his clay into a sausage. 'Ooh it's very calming, isn't it,' he said.

And then he stopped rolling.

'What's up, Mr Plonsky?' asked Yoshi, who's the sort of person who notices a floating sausage of clay suddenly stop being rolled.

'What are those things?' said Terry, pointing to the shelf at the back of the room.

Not that the others could see where his invisible finger was pointing.

Rhubarb looked around the room. Lined up at the back of it, next to Mrs Terrible, were about fifty small pottery animals. They had long tails, short legs and ginormous smiles.

'Crocodiles!' cried Terry. 'They're clay crocodiles!'

Mrs Terrible banged her fist on her desk. 'Keep it down, I said!'

Melvin put his hand up. 'Erm, excuse me, Mrs Terrible. Who made those things?'

'Me, of course,' snarled the miserable woman, picking one of the crocodiles up and throwing it against the wall. It smashed into a million pieces.

'What's it got to do with you?'

'Crikey, she really is terrible,' whispered Terry.

Melvin stroked his chin, Rhubarb-style. 'There's something fishy going on here,' he said. 'Or should I say, CROCODILEY.'

'You're not suggesting . . .' said Yoshi.

Melvin smiled. 'Maybe I am.'

Rhubarb stared at her friends. 'What are you talking about?'

Melvin did his serious face. 'I think Mrs Terrible might have something to do with your dad being eaten by that you-know-what.'

Rhubarb sniffed the air. 'What, just because she made a few crocodiles out of clay? I'm afraid I'm not smelling it, Melv.'

Terry's sausage stopped being rolled again. 'Uh, oh,' he said. 'I think I've spotted something else as well.'

Yoshi held his pencil a millimetre above his notepad. 'What have you seen now, Mr P?'

'Mrs Terrible's teeth,' said Terry.

'What about them?' asked Rhubarb.

Terry scratched his bum and reappeared with a grin on his face.

'Meet me in the next chapter and I'll tell you,' he said, giving his left buttock an itch and disappearing again.

Very short teeth

'Have you noticed how short and jaggedy Mrs Terrible's teeth are?' said Terry, once the next chapter had started.

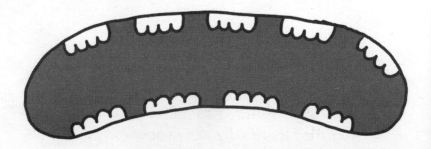

Rhubarb zoomed in on the lady's gnashers. She had to admit, they were pretty short and jaggedy. 'So what if they are, though?' she asked.

Melvin gasped. 'Maybe she bought a SUCK & BRUSH!' he said.

Terry squidged his lump of clay into a really rubbish thumbs-up. 'Exactly what I was thinking, Melv,' he said.

'I don't get it,' said Yoshi.

'Maybe all the fizzy drink wore her teeth down to little stumps,' said Melvin. 'Maybe she fed Mr Plonsky to the crocodile for ruining her smile.'

'I suppose it's possible...' said Rhubarb. 'But even if the SUCK & BRUSH did ruin Mrs Terrible's teeth, would she really bother tracking down the inventor?'

Terry shrugged. 'It'd explain those pottery crocodiles,' he said.

Rhubarb frowned. 'I don't see why she'd be making loads of pottery crocodiles just because she fed you to one. Besides, wouldn't it be a bit of a giveaway?'

Melvin clicked his fingers. 'Yes!' he said.

SPORT

DONUT POTTERY

DO

Rhubarb smiled. It wasn't often people realised how stupid they'd been sounding, just by listening to you explain it to them.

'I'm glad you see my point, Melv,' she said.

Melvin scrunched his face up. 'What point?' he said. 'No, I was just thinking of that note your dad had in his lunchbox . . . it had the letter T at the bottom, remember?' He pointed at Mrs Terrible. 'T for TERRIBLE!'

Mrs Terrible, who was squidging a lump of clay into the shape of another crocodile, looked up. 'What are you lot jabbering on about now?' she snapped, like she was one herself.

'Nothing, Mrs Terrible,' said Rhubarb, turning to her friends. 'Okay, so we have one theory. But I really do think we should pop down to Donut Zoo where the whole thing happened.'

Yoshi looked at the wonky teacup he'd been making. 'I'm up for that,' he said.

Terry went quiet for a second. 'I suppose a trip to the zoo might be nice.'

'Oh come on then,' said Melvin. 'But I'm telling you, it's a waste of time.'

Donut Zoo

They paid Mrs Terrible and strolled across town until they got to a big entrance with 'Donut Zoo' written above it.

Melvin sighed. 'Why did I go along with this?' he said. 'We should be back in Donut Pottery interviewing Mrs Terrible.'

A little man sitting inside a little booth
next to the entrance tapped on its window.
'Welcome to Donut Zoo!' he called.
'Can I help you?'

Rhubarb zoomed her eyes in on the little
man's name tag. 'Mr Really Nice,' she said,
reading what was on it.

'Funny old name for a man sitting in a
booth,' said Terry, and the man blinked.

'Blimey, one of you's got a very deep
voice,' he said.

Melvin coughed. 'That was me,' he said. 'I think I swallowed a frog at lunchtime.'

'Oh, right,' said Mr Really Nice, doing a chuckle. 'Well in that case I won't show you the way to the amphibian house. We don't want you eating any of our exhibits, do we.'

Rhubarb stroked her chin. 'Funny you should say that, because we're looking for a crocodile.'

'Oh, they're in the reptile house,' said Mr Really Nice. 'Just next door to the amphibians.'

'Amphibians, reptiles, what's the difference,' said Terry, and Melvin coughed again.

Yoshi pointed at Rhubarb. 'Her dad got eaten by one when she was a baby,' he said.

'A frog?' said Mr Really Nice.

'No, a crocodile,' said Yoshi.

Mr Really Nice gasped. 'So you're little Rhubarb Plonsky,' he said. 'I'm so sorry about what happened to your father all those years ago.'

'Thanks,' said Rhubarb, winking at her dad. 'So, about that reptile house . . .'

Mr Really Nice whipped a fold-up map out of a little holder and pointed at a drawing of the entrance. 'We're here,' he said. 'To get to the reptile house you need to go up this path and turn right at the hippo enclosure.'

There was a drawing of a hippo's bum on the map. 'Our hippo has the fattest bum in the whole of Donut,' said Mr Really Nice, all proudly.

'Very impressive,' said Yoshi.

'Next you have to go past the giraffes,' said Mr Really Nice, pointing at a drawing of a giraffe. 'That's Longy Long Neck,' he said. 'He's got the longest neck in the whole of Donut.'

'You don't say,' said Melvin.

Mr Really Nice carried on with his mini tour. 'Then take a left at the meerkats,' he said.

This time, the drawing on the map was of a wooden cut-out meerkat. 'Largest wooden cut-out of a meerkat on the island,' said Mr Really Nice.

Rhubarb chuckled. 'I never knew,' she said.

117

'Finally, you walk through the bat cave,' said Mr Really Nice. 'Then you're at the Reptile House.'

Yoshi put his hand up. 'Don't tell me, it's the biggest bat cave in Donut, right?'

Mr Really Nice shook his head. 'No, the smallest,' he said. 'And very proud of it we are too.'

Crocodile Tony

The gang said thanks to Mr Really Nice and followed his ridonkulous directions.

When they got to the reptile house, the first thing Rhubarb spotted was a man sweeping up poo.

Pinned on to his jumper was a name tag with the words 'Crocodile Tony' written on it.

Crocodile Tony was in the middle of a cage just about the right size for a Komodo dragon. Which made sense seeing as there was a Komodo dragon standing next to him.

Either side of the cage were two larger cages, one for a friendly-looking family of tortoises and the other for a pair of bored-looking crocodiles.

Crocodile Tony peered over at the kids.
'What are you looking at?' he growled.
He certainly didn't seem as nice as
Mr Really Nice.

Rhubarb handed Crocodile Tony one of her
business cards. 'We're from The Daily Donut,'
she said. 'Wondered if we could ask you a
few questions.'

Rhubarb Plonsky
Editor, The Daily Donut

ll Mysteries Investigated

'About what?' snapped Crocodile Tony,
all crocodilishly.

Rhubarb sniffed the air, which smelt of
Komodo dragon poo. 'Does the name
Terry Plonsky ring any bells?'

Crocodile Tony's eyes went all wide, like a chameleon's. 'The Grabby Grabber man,' he muttered.

'The Grabby Grabber man?' said Terry. 'That's a funny old name for me.'

Crocodile Tony looked around. 'Who said that?'

Melvin coughed. 'Sorry, I ate a frog for lunch,' he said.

AS SEEN ON PAGE 113!

'Oh right,' said Crocodile Tony, like that was a completely normal thing to do.

Rhubarb stared at him. 'Excuse me, Crocodile Tony, but why did you just call my dad the Grabby Grabber man?'

Crocodile Tony blinked. 'Don't tell me you're his little girl,' he said. 'I remember you from that day . . . you were only a baby then, of course.'

A shiver went down Rhubarb's spine, like in a book when somebody's been spooked. 'What day?' she asked.

'The day I met your father,' said Crocodile Tony. 'He was here with you and your mum.'

'What were we doing in Donut Zoo?' asked Rhubarb.

Crocodile Tony shrugged. 'Just having a day out, I suppose.'

'What, and my dad had a Grabby Grabber with him?' asked Rhubarb.

'Oh no,' said Crocodile Tony. 'But he was telling me all about it. Thought it might come in handy when I was feeding the crocodiles.'

'That was thoughtful of him,' said Yoshi.

'Yeah,' said Crocodile Tony. 'Anyway, he said he'd bring along a Grabby Grabber for me the next day.' He looked down and shook his head.

'And what happened?' asked Rhubarb. She had a horrible feeling she already knew the answer.

Crocodile Tony sighed. 'I was late for our meeting,' he said. 'Too late.'

Yoshi looked up from his notepad. 'What do you mean, Crocodile Tony?'

'By the time I got here, all that was left of the Grabby Grabber man was his lunchbox,' said Crocodile Tony.

* Long time no see!

'The crocodile had eaten him,' said Yoshi.
He glanced at the big cage with the
two bored-looking crocodiles inside.
'But how did it happen?'

Crocodile Tony scratched his bum, but didn't
disappear. 'Who knows,' he said.

Rhubarb put her hand up, like she was in
Mr Thursday's classroom. 'What about my dad's
Grabby Grabber?' she asked. 'Wasn't that there
too?'

'Hmm, that's a point,' said Crocodile Tony, looking like he was flicking through his brain. 'No, it wasn't.'

Yoshi scribbled this fact down as Rhubarb stroked her chin. 'Very interesting,' she said. 'I wonder where it disappeared off to.'

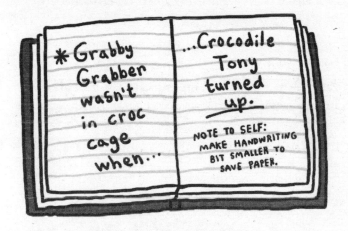

Melvin sighed. 'Are we finished here yet?' he said. 'Because I really wanna get back to Donut Pottery.'

'Just one more thing,' said Rhubarb to Crocodile Tony. 'Which one of those two crocs swallowed my dad? I'd like to interview him.'

Crocodile Tony did a chuckle. 'Interview a crocodile?' he said. 'That's a bit weird, innit?'

Melvin rolled his eyes. 'Yeah, she's like that,' he said.

Crocodile Tony blinked. 'I'm afraid Ray isn't with us any more,' he said to Rhubarb.

He pointed to the wall behind the crocodile cage. Slap bang in the middle was a little plaque with a picture of a crocodile on it.

'In memory of Ray the crocodile,' it said.

'Ray,' Terry mumbled to himself. 'Funny old name for a crocodile.'

'He's buried in Donut Pet Cemetery now,' said Mr Really Nice.

'Donut Pet Cemetery, you say,' said Rhubarb, turning round and heading towards the exit.

'Yeah that's right,' said Crocodile Tony.

'Donut Pet Cemetery.

Nice little title for a chapter that, innit.'

"DONUT PET CEMETERY"

The words above the entrance to Donut Pet Cemetery were exactly the same as the ones above Donut Zoo's, except they said 'Donut Pet Cemetery'. Oh yeah, and they were made out of bones.

'This place gives me the creeps,' said Yoshi, peering around for a crocodiley-looking gravestone.

Terry leaned against a statue of a cat and stared into the distance.

'You alright, Dad?' asked Rhubarb. He'd been quiet the whole way there.

'Yeah I'm fine,' said Terry, scratching his bum and reappearing. 'Just feels a bit weird being in a cemetery, that's all.'

'I thought you'd feel at home,' said Yoshi. 'What with you being dead and everything.'

'Thanks for that,' said Terry. The ghostified chocolate bar loop-the-looped in the air above his head and he grabbed it, taking a bite.

'Hey, look at this one,' called Melvin. He was standing by a gravestone the size of an ice lolly.

'Jerby the Terrible,' said Yoshi, strolling over and reading what was carved into it. Under that it said, 'Best pet gerbil ever.'

Melvin gasped. 'It's got to be Mrs Terrible's gerbil,' he said, pointing at the word 'Terrible'.

'Wouldn't he just be called "Jerby Terrible" then?' said Rhubarb, but Melvin ignored her.

'New theory,' he said. 'Mrs Terrible accidentally trod on her pet gerbil while wearing a pair of TRAINER TRAINERS.'

Terry stroked his chin. 'Her revenge was feeding me to Ray the crocodile . . .' he said. 'I like it!'

Rhubarb looked at Melvin and her dad, trying to decide which one of them was being more of an idiot.

'Hey you lot,' cried Yoshi, who'd wandered off. 'I think I've found Ray!'

They all ran over and looked at the gravestone. 'Ray the crocodile,' said the words on it. Stuffed into a little vase in front of the gravestone were some freshly cut flowers.

'I wonder who put those there,' said Yoshi.

Rhubarb thought for a second. 'Crocodile Tony, maybe?'

Melvin shook his head. 'I reckon it was Mrs Terrible,' he said. 'As a thank you to Ray for eating your dad.'

Rhubarb turned to Melvin. 'So why didn't she put any on Jerby the Terrible's grave, then?'

Melvin rolled his eyes. 'Don't be silly,' he said. 'That'd give the whole game away!'

Terry pointed at Melvin. 'Now that's smart thinking.'

'Oh yeah, Melvin's a regular genius,' said Rhubarb. She was beginning to get a little bit fed up with him and her dad's stupid ideas.

Melvin looked at his next-door neighbour and sniffed the air, the way she always did. 'Are you being sarcastic?' he asked.

'Yes I am,' said Rhubarb. 'I mean, are you even listening to yourself?'

'Of course I'm listening to myself,' said Melvin. 'Have you seen how close my ears are to my mouth?'

2cm

Rhubarb tried to think of something clever to say about the distance between Melvin's ears and mouth, but all she could come up with was, 'Not far enough,' which didn't even make any sense.

Terry did the time out sign with his see-through hands. 'Time out,' he said, because nobody does the time out sign without saying 'time out' as well, do they? 'Come on you two, this isn't worth arguing over.'

'Yeah,' said Yoshi. 'Why ruin a friendship over how far someone's ears are from their mouth?'

Rhubarb scrunched her face up. 'It's got nothing to do with that. I just think Melvin's wrong about Mrs Terrible.'

'So what's your amazing theory then?' snapped Melvin.

'ENOUGH!'

shouted Terry, and Rhubarb jumped.

'Relax, Dad,' she said. 'We're just having a little disagreement. It's what detectives do.'

Terry smiled at his daughter. 'Sorry Rubes,' he said. 'You two arguing like that reminded me of something, that's all.'

'You remembered something?' said Rhubarb. 'That's great! Was it to do with the crocodile?'

Terry shook his head. 'No, nothing to do with that,' he said.

'Oh,' said Rhubarb, her nose drooping.

'What was it, then?' asked Yoshi.

'My first ever invention,' said Terry.

Rhubarb looked at her dad. 'What about your first invention?'

Terry stared into the distance. 'You don't even want to know,' he said, all mysteriously.

Barnaby Toenails

You know when somebody says, 'You don't even want to know,' and it makes everyone really, really want to know? That's what happened next.

'Tell us about your invention, Mr Plonsky,' said Yoshi. 'Pleeease!'

Terry shook his head, and Rhubarb's see-through snacks shook theirs too. 'Oh, it was nothing,' he said.

'Nothing stories are my favourite!' said
Rhubarb. 'Come on, Dad. It might even help
us crack the case.'

Melvin scoffed. 'I seriously doubt it,' he said.

'Well,' said Terry. 'I had a friend called
Barnaby when I was kid. Barnaby Toenails.'

Melvin laughed. 'Barnaby Toenails? I thought
Rhubarb had a silly name!'

'Your name isn't so great either, PEBBLES!'
said Rhubarb.

Terry ignored them and carried on with his
story. 'Barnaby was my next-door neighbour,'
he said. 'We did everything together.'

Rhubarb blinked. 'What, you went to the toilet together?' she asked.

'Sometimes,' said Terry. 'Only wees though, not poos.'

Yoshi giggled. 'Carry on, Mr P,' he said.

'Barnaby was always round my house,' said Terry. 'Whatever I did, he did it too.'

'Sounds familiar,' said Rhubarb, looking
at Melvin.

Terry chuckled to himself, like he'd just
remembered something else. 'I got a lovely
new jumper once,' he said. 'It had a lightning
bolt on the front.'

Melvin leaned over to Rhubarb. 'Skip to the
end,' he whispered.

'The next day, Barnaby turned up at my front
door wearing the exact same thing,' said Terry.

'What a copier!' said Melvin.

'Yeah, I got ever so annoyed with him for that,' said Terry. 'Shouldn't have really, it was only a jumper.'

Yoshi patted Terry on the shoulder, his hand disappearing into it. 'Don't beat yourself up about it, Mr P.'

Terry's eyes went all fuzzy. 'I always wanted to be an inventor,' he said, as if he was only just realising it for the first time. 'Of course, Barnaby wanted to be one as well.'

'This is great, Dad,' said Rhubarb. 'You're really starting to remember stuff now.'

Terry smiled. 'There was a school science fair. I was working on a Shrink Ray Gun for it.'

'A Shrink Ray Gun?' said Yoshi. 'Not an actual real life one?'

'I showed Barnaby what I was making,' said Terry, completely ignoring Yoshi's question. 'He thought it was the best thing ever. "Let's work on it together," he said. But I wanted to do it all by myself.'

'There's nothing wrong with that,' said Melvin.

Terry shrugged. 'Finally it was the morning of the science fair. I'd brought along my Shrink Ray Gun and a can of Donut Soda.'

'Mmm, Donut soda,' said Melvin. 'My mum won't let me drink it, of course.'

Yoshi looked up from his notepad. 'This Shrink Ray Gun,' he said. 'It wasn't actually a real life one, was it?'

Once again, Terry ignored his question. 'I'd just set up my stall when Barnaby arrived. He was carrying a great big cardboard box.'

'Let me guess what was inside,' said Melvin. 'A Shrink Ray Gun.'

Terry nodded.

'How did that make you feel, Dad?' asked Rhubarb.

'I couldn't believe it,' said Terry. 'I mean, copying my jumper was one thing, but my whole blooming science project?'

'It's just not on,' said Melvin.

'What was worse, Barnaby was up first,' said Terry.

'But then the judges would think you'd copied him!' said Yoshi.

Rhubarb looked at her dad. 'So what did you do?'

'One word,' said Terry. 'Logo.'

'Logo?' said Melvin. 'What logo?'

'I pointed at the logo on Barnaby's Shrink Ray Gun,' said Terry.

Rhubarb rewound her brain to the day before, when she'd been working on a new logo for The Daily Donut. 'Don't tell me he copied the logo on your Shrink Ray Gun,' she said.

'I ran over to Barnaby and grabbed his gun then turned it upside down,' said Terry. 'There, on the bottom of it, were some tiny little letters.'

'What did they say?' asked Yoshi.

Rhubarb smiled. 'Let me guess - 'Made in Donut'. And the O was a donut, right?'

Terry nodded. 'All I had to do then was show the judges a few of my other inventions. They all had the same logo on them.'

Yoshi was writing everything down. 'And what did the judges say, Mr P?'

'Barnaby was disqualified from the competition.'

'Serves him right,' said Melvin.

Terry shrugged. 'I suppose,' he said. 'Anyway, then it was my turn. I pointed the Shrink Ray Gun at the can and squeezed the trigger.'

'Did it work?' asked Rhubarb.

'Well, the can disappeared,' said Terry.

Yoshi gasped. 'You shrunk the Donut Soda?
So it WAS a real life Shrink Ray Gun!'

'Not exactly,' said Terry.

Melvin blinked. 'What did it do, then?'

Terry did a little explosion with his hands.

he said. 'It blew it to smithereens.'

After that

'So you're saying the Shrink Ray Gun didn't work?' asked Yoshi.

Terry sighed. 'It was a complete and utter failure.'

'What happened with you and Barnaby?' asked Rhubarb.

'A few months later his family moved across town to the Smelly Side,' said Terry.

'The Smelly Side,' said Melvin. 'People are weird over there.'

Rhubarb put her hand on her dad's see-through shoulder, and her fingers sank into it. 'I take it you and him stopped being friends after that.'

'Pretty much,' said Terry, smiling at her and Melvin. 'I just don't want that happening to you two.'

Rhubarb looked at her next-door neighbour. He was stroking his chin the way she always did.

Maybe he was her version of Barnaby Toenails, she thought to herself.

'Don't you worry about me and Rubes, Mr P,' said Melvin. 'We'll be OK.'

Rhubarb nodded. 'Did you ever see Barnaby again?' she asked her dad. 'It's just, I was wondering . . .'

Terry scratched his bum and disappeared. 'Erm, no. No, I didn't,' he said.

'What were you wondering, Rubes?' asked Yoshi.

Terry scratched his bum again and reappeared. 'Anyone else feeling a bit pooped?' he said, stretching his arms out and yawning. 'Reckon we should be heading off.'

'Good idea,' said Melvin. 'Maybe we could pop into Donut Pottery and have a little chat with Mrs Terrible on the way home.'

'Seriously?' said Rhubarb. 'You're still going on about her?'

Melvin nodded. 'Why not? Anyway, I've got a new theory.'

Terry rubbed his hands together. 'Ooh lovely, let's hear it, Melv.'

Yoshi put his hand up. 'But I wanted to hear what Rhubarb was thinking.'

Rhubarb shook her head. 'Forget it, Yosh,' she said. Her dad was obviously more interested in Melvin's ideas than hers.

'Come on then,' said Terry, smiling at Melvin. 'I'm all ears.'

'It's about this Shrink Ray Gun of yours,' said Melvin. 'I think Mrs Terrible might've been trying to get her hands on one.'

'For what?' Rhubarb laughed. 'So she could shrink her teacups down to dolls' house size?'

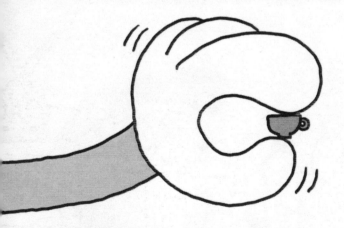

Melvin scoffed. 'Don't be silly. I haven't worked it out yet, but I'm sure it fits together somehow.'

Terry stroked his chin, and Rhubarb wondered if that's where she got it from. 'It's an interesting theory, that's for sure,' he said.

'No it's not!' cried Rhubarb. Why did her dad keep thinking Melvin's stupid ideas were so good? 'I've had enough of this.' She started to walk home.

They headed back down Donut High Street, the pavement still all squidgy.

'Oh well that's just brilliant,' said Melvin, pointing across the road to Donut Pottery. 'It's closed!'

Terry, who'd scratched his bum and gone invisible again, smiled. 'Don't worry Melv, there's always tomorrow.'

Tomorrow, thought Rhubarb. That was the deadline for the Newshound Award, and they were nowhere near solving their mystery.

'See you in the morning then,' said Yoshi, when they got to Rhubarb and Melvin's houses.

Melvin walked up to his door. 'Bright and early,' he said. 'Something tells me it's not going to be a good day for Mrs Terrible.'

Mum's the word

Rhubarb ignored her annoying next-door neighbour and smiled at her dad. 'Wait until Mum sees you,' she said, pulling the front door key out of her pocket. 'She won't believe her eyes!'

Terry just floated there, all invisible. 'About that,' he whispered. 'Do you mind if we keep it to ourselves for now?'

Rhubarb's nose drooped. 'But don't you want to say hello?' asked Rhubarb.

'Course I do,' said Terry.

'Then scratch your bum!' said Rhubarb.

'Listen, Rubes,' said Terry. 'You'll have to trust me on this one.'

Just then, the front door opened. 'I thought that was you,' said Thelma, smiling down at Rhubarb. 'Who were you talking to?'

'Oh nobody,' said Rhubarb, grinning up at her mum like an idiot. 'Just myself. There's no one else here, honest.'

Her mum blinked. 'How was your day?'

'Interesting . . .' said Rhubarb, trying to work out what to say. 'Oh yeah, The Daily Donut's been nominated for the Newshound Award.'

'That's amazing!' said her mum. 'What are you going to write about?'

Rhubarb thought for a second. 'Erm, well, there's something weird going on with the pavements around town. Maybe we'll look into that.'

Thelma gave her a cuddle. 'My little detective! Your dad would be so proud.'

'Do you really think?' asked Rhubarb, going into the living room and slumping on to the sofa.

'Definitely,' whispered Terry, flomping down next to her.

Thelma scrunched her face up. 'Did you hear that?' she said, plonking her bum down on the other side of her daughter.

'What?' said Rhubarb, happy to be squidged between her mum and dad for the first time she could remember. 'I didn't hear anything.'

'I could've sworn someone was whispering,' said Thelma.

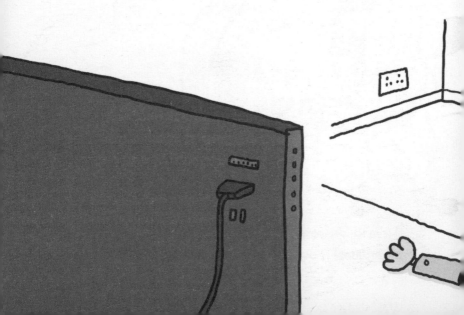

Rhubarb glanced around for the remote control. As usual, it was on the other side of the room.

She spotted the Grabby Grabber, sitting on the coffee table, and leaned forwards to grab it, wondering again where the one in Donut Zoo could have disappeared to.

Donut Pizza

Rhubarb woke up on Saturday morning with her phone ringing. She reached over and slid her finger across the screen.

'Get down to Donut Pizza right now,' crackled Melvin's voice, then he hung up.

Rhubarb jumped out of bed. 'Ow!' cried Terry, who was curled up on the floor, Yoshi's little ghost book lying on the carpet next to him.

'Sorry, Dad,' said Rhubarb. 'That was Melvin, he's down Donut Pizza.'

'Ooh, has he got a new lead?' asked Terry, picking up the book and slotting it into his pocket.

'He probably thinks he has,' said Rhubarb, grabbing her rucksack with the lunchbox still inside.

Terry yawned. He snatched the ghostified satsuma floating above his head and peeled its skin off in one go. 'Melvin's not stupid, you know,' he said, chomping on a segment.

Rhubarb rolled her eyes. 'I know he's not. It's just . . . you don't actually think Mrs Terrible could have fed you to that crocodile, do you?'

'Anything's possible,' said Terry. He scratched his bum and disappeared.

Another firework exploded inside Rhubarb's tummy, except this was one of those really annoying whiny ones that go on for too long then fizzle without a bang.

How could my clever old dad be so stupid, she thought to herself.

'Come on, let's get some fresh air,' she said, heading out the door.

They strolled down to Donut Pizza in silence. When they got there, they squidged into the booth next to Melvin and Yoshi.

Two completely full-up glasses of tap water sat on the table in front of them. 'I love this place,' said Melvin. 'You don't even have to buy a drink!'

Rhubarb glanced around and spotted a familiar trio sitting in a booth on the other side of the room. 'Oh great, just what I need. The Cool Doods.'

Hector twizzled his head like it was a tin of baked beans and looked at Rhubarb.

'What has he got, super hearing or something?' she muttered to herself.

Hector smiled. 'Found anything to investigate yet, losers?' he said. 'We've pretty much cracked our case, haven't we, Doods?'

Dirk and Marjorie nodded as they slurped on their breakfast colas.

'Good for you,' said Rhubarb, not that she meant it. She really needed to get a move on with this mystery.

Just then, the owner of Donut Pizza, who had 'Hi, I'm Steven' written on his name tag, trudged over to The Daily Donut's table. 'Hi, I'm Steven,' he said. 'Can I get you guys anything to eat?'

'Do you mind, Steven?' said Melvin. 'I've got some important news to tell my friend.'

'Ever so sorry, sir,' said Steven, turning round on the spot.

'Don't go, Steven!' said Rhubarb, feeling a bit sorry for him, and he rotated again. Rhubarb glanced at the menu. 'Erm, I'll have a Breakfast Pizza, please.'

Steven tapped it into his little machine. 'One Breakfast Pizza coming right up!' he said.

'Check it out,' said Melvin, handing Rhubarb a pair of binoculars. She peered through them at Donut Pottery across the street.

'What am I looking at, exactly?' asked Rhubarb. She could see Mrs Terrible working on another pottery crocodile.

'We followed her to work this morning,' said Melvin. 'Mrs Terrible was taking photos of dogs the whole way,' said Melvin.

Rhubarb shrugged. 'So what?'

Yoshi looked up from his notepad. 'Melvin thinks Mrs Terrible's looking for the perfect dog.'

'For what?' asked Rhubarb.

'To feed her next victim to,' said Melvin, all seriously. 'She's a monster and we have to stop her RIGHT NOW!'

'That's it,' said Rhubarb, scraping out of her chair.

'Where are you off to?' asked Terry.

'The Smelly Side, to look for Barnaby Toenails,' said Rhubarb. 'I'm not wasting any more time here.'

Melvin scoffed. 'Barnaby Toenails? What's he got to do with anything?'

'Don't go, Rubes,' said Terry.

Rhubarb looked at her dad, not that she could see him. 'Why not?'

'Erm, I think I might be remembering something very important all of a sudden,' he said. 'Something that could help you crack the case.'

Rhubarb squinted her eyes. 'You know, sometimes it feels like you're actually trying to STOP me cracking it.'

'Ha ha.' said Terry. 'Why would I do that?'

Yoshi whipped his notepad out and hovered his pencil a millimetre above the page. 'Tell us what you remember, Mr P.'

'One word,' said Terry.

And then he said the word.

Bogeynose™

'Bogeynose,' said Yoshi, writing down the word Terry had just said. 'Hey, I used to have one of those!'

'Mmm, Bogeynoses,' said Melvin. 'My mum never let me have one, of course.'

Rhubarb remembered the first time she'd tried a Bogeynose, and smiled. 'I forgot you invented them.'

A Bogeynose, in case you've never seen one, is tiny little vending machine that slots over your hooter. It picks your bogeys and adds a different flavour to each one. Then you press a button and they pop out, straight on to your tongue.

'So what about them, anyway?' said Rhubarb, looking at her watch. 'I haven't got all day, you know.'

Terry went quiet for a second. 'Well, I was just thinking,' he said. 'Maybe Mrs Terrible didn't like her kid eating their own bogies...'

Rhubarb sighed. 'And let me guess, she fed you to the crocodile as revenge?'

Terry nodded, or at least it sounded like he did.

'That's the worst idea yet,' said Rhubarb. 'You're as bad as Melvin.'

'Come on, Rubes,' said Terry. 'Think about it for a second.'

Rhubarb thought for a second. 'There,' she said. 'I've thought about it and it's still completely stupid.'

Just then, Steven appeared carrying a
Breakfast Pizza. 'One Breakfast Pizza,'
he said, placing it carefully on the table.
'I hope you enjoy it.'

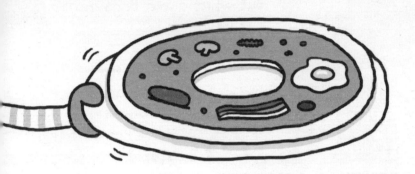

'Ooh, it's got a hole in the middle!' said Terry.
'So that's why it's called Donut Pizza.'

'Who said that?' said Steven, looking around.

Melvin coughed. 'That was me,' he said, in a
deep voice. 'Thank you, Steven, that'll be all
for now.'

Steven backed away, slowly.

'You can't go now Rubes,' whispered Terry. 'Look, there's a whole Breakfast Pizza to eat. And it's got a hole in the middle!'

Rhubarb grabbed a slice and slotted it into her mouth. 'I'll have it to go.'

'But what about Bogeynose?' said Terry.

'What about it?' said Rhubarb. 'The whole idea's completely stupid.'

'You know, Rubes,' said Melvin, stroking his chin. 'You'll never crack this case if you keep telling people their ideas are stupid.'

'Yeah well, you'll never crack it because you're a rubbish detective!' cried Rhubarb. 'And by the way, stop copying the way I stroke my chin.'

'That's not very nice, Rubes,' said Yoshi.

Rhubarb shrugged. 'Maybe I'm not very nice sometimes. But at least I don't waste my time coming up with crazy ideas that don't get me anywhere!'

'Of course you're nice,' said Terry. 'You're the nicest girl in the whole wide world.'

Rhubarb looked at her dad. 'And I used to think you were the cleverest dad on the whole of Donut Island,' she said, marching towards the door. 'But now I'm not so sure.'

The Copiers

Rhubarb pushed the door open and stepped on to Donut High Street. 'Let's see what the Smelly Side has to say for itself,' she muttered to herself.

Just then, the door opened behind her. Rhubarb turned around, hoping it might be her dad. After all, she hadn't really meant what she'd said. She was just annoyed he kept taking Melvin's side.

'I wonder if we could have a quick word,' said Hector Frisbee, and Rhubarb's nose drooped.

'Oh, it's you lot,' she said, starting to walk off in the direction of the Smelly Side.

The Cool Doods followed behind her. 'Don't sound so disappointed,' said Hector. 'You haven't heard what I've got to say yet.'

'Go on then,' said Rhubarb, her nostrils waggling with curiosity. 'I'm all ears.'

Hector chuckled. 'Funny you should say that,' he said, patting his left ear. 'Because so am I.'

Rhubarb scrunched her face up. What was he talking about? 'Just get on with it, Frisbee. I've got a Newshound Award to win.'

'So have we,' said Hector. 'In fact, we're this close to cracking The Mysterious Case Of How Your Dad Ended Up Inside His Self-Packing Lunchbox. No thanks to Melvin and his ridonkulous ideas.'

Hector turned his head and smiled, his left ear facing Rhubarb's eyes. Sticking out of the earhole was a little plastic earpiece with a tiny satellite dish attached to it.

Rhubarb gasped. 'You're wearing an EAR BUG!'
she cried.

'You cracked it,' said Hector, tapping his earlobe,
and the tiny dish swivelled around until it was
pointing at a lamppost a few metres away.
'I can actually hear an ant climbing up that
lamppost, you know. Isn't that amazing?'

'Yeah I know, my dad invented them,' said
Rhubarb. 'Are you telling me you've been
listening in on us this whole time?'

Hector nodded. 'And very entertaining it's
been, too.'

'But I thought you had your own top secret
mystery to solve?' said Rhubarb.

'Nah, we made that up,' said Marjorie.
'Couldn't have you thinking you were gonna
beat us, could we?'

'So you copied ours instead,' said Rhubarb.
'You're as bad as Barnaby Toenails!'

Hector laughed. 'I wouldn't go that far,' he said.

Rhubarb rewound her brain to the afternoon
before. 'So you heard what we were saying in
Donut Pottery?'

'Loud and clear,' said Dirk. 'We were just
across the road in Donut Pizza, remember?'

'And Donut Zoo?' asked Rhubarb.

Marjorie nodded.

'We had a lovely day out, didn't we, Doods?' she said, pointing at a badge stuck on to her jumper.

'She didn't really cuddle a koala,' said Dirk. 'That badge is a complete liar.'

I CUDDLED A KOALA AT DONUT ZOO!

Hector grinned at Rhubarb. 'After Donut Zoo we had a nice stroll through Donut Pet Cemetery. I have to say, we agreed with everything you said.'

Dirk pulled his notepad out. 'Yeah, what was that Melvin loser talking about?' he said, flicking through it. 'As if Mrs Terrible fed your dad to Ray the crocodile!'

'I know, right?' said Rhubarb. Then she remembered who she was talking to.

She turned and marched off.

The Cool Doods carried on following her. 'We like the way you're going about the whole investigation,' said Hector. 'And we wondered . . .'

'Wondered what?' said Rhubarb.

She was pretty sure she knew what was coming next.

Hector smiled. 'We wondered if you fancied working together,' he said.

They were walking round the massive hole in the middle of the island now. Rhubarb stared into it, remembering the giant slime monster that'd climbed out and tried to eat her and her pals.

'What's in it for me?' she said. 'Apart from hanging out with the amazing Cool Doods, of course.'

Dirk shrugged. 'We just thought you could do with a bit of help,' he said. 'Don't you want to win the Newshound Award?'

Marjorie nodded. 'Yeah, cos you're never going to while that lot's going along with Melvin's stupid ideas.'

Rhubarb pictured Melvin and Yoshi, sitting in Donut Pizza with her dad, staring through the binoculars at Mrs Terrible.

She stared into the hole again and sighed.

'Follow me,' she said. 'There's no time to lose.'

BACK TO THE "SMELLY" "SIDE"

Rhubarb sniffed the stinky air. It was five minutes later and she and The Cool Doods were standing on the Smelly Side of Donut Island.

Dirk pinched his nose. 'What's the plan, boss?' he asked Hector.

Rhubarb tried to think. What was she even doing, hanging out with this lot? Well, at least they listened to her ideas.

'Now we find Barnaby Toenails,' she said.

They strolled on to the High Street and glanced around. 'What does this Barnaby Toenails fellow look like, then?' asked Hector.

Rhubarb frowned.
'That's the problem.
I have absolutely
no idea.'

Across the road stood
Smelly Side Supermarket.

'But I do know the
manager of that
place. Maybe she
can help.'

The glass doors whooshed open and they
stepped inside. Straightaway Rhubarb
spotted a twizzled-round packet of Elbow
Rash cream, sitting on a shelf.

'Aren't you that Celery girl from The Daily
Donut?' said a familiar voice, and Gloria
appeared from behind a pyramid of
enormous glass jars.

'It's Rhubarb, not Celery,' said Rhubarb, staring at the jars. Inside each one floated about fifteen humungous gherkins.

'You don't need any courgettes, do you?' asked Gloria. 'I can't get rid of the blooming things.'

Rhubarb shook her head. 'Not right now, thanks,' she said, pointing at the elbow cream. 'I see the Phantom Twizzler's back.'

Gloria groaned. 'The man's a menace. What are you doing here, anyway?'

'There's something you might be able to help me with,' said Rhubarb.

Gloria leaned against the pyramid and the whole thing wobbled. 'I'm all ears,' she said.

'Barnaby Toenails,' said Rhubarb. 'That name doesn't ring any bells, does it?'

Gloria scratched her head. 'Can't say it does. Is this another one of your mysteries?'

Rhubarb nodded. 'I think he might've fed my dad to a crocodile.'

'Ah ha!' said Hector. 'So that's your theory is it, Plonsky?'

Gloria blinked. 'Fed your dad to a crocodile?
He doesn't sound very nice.'

Just then, Rhubarb heard a familiar beeping sound.
She looked up and spotted the Phantom Twizzler,
standing next to the pyramid of giant gherkins.

'Oi, you're banned!' screamed Gloria.

'ARGH!' cried Hector, grabbing his left ear. 'Not
so loud, lady. Some of us are wearing EAR BUGS!'

The Phantom Twizzler cackled. 'I told you I'd be back!' he said, picking up a giant jar with his Grabby Grabber. 'Cor blimey, these gherkins are whoppers, aren't they.'

GRAB!

Gloria sighed. 'Tell me about it,' she said. 'Now get out of my supermarket!'

Marjorie pointed at the jar. 'What you need is a Shrink Ray for those things,' she said to Gloria.

Dirk peered down at his notepad. 'I think you'll find it's a 'Shrink Ray GUN',' he said, trying to read his scribbly handwriting.

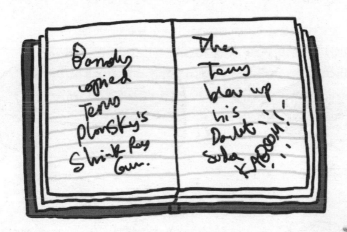

'Yeah, but Shrink RAY sounds much better,' said Marjorie. 'More snappy.'

Rhubarb's eyes opened wide. 'Shrink Ray,' she whispered to herself, turning to look at the Phantom Twizzler's Grabby Grabber. 'That's it!'

'What's what?' grumbled Hector, rubbing his left ear.

'Oh, erm, nothing,' said Rhubarb. 'False alarm.'

Hector scrunched his face up. 'Is there something you're not telling me, Plonsky?'

'No,' said Rhubarb, even though there was. All of a sudden, she wished her real friends were there.

'Hmm,' said Hector, pulling his EAR BUG out and giving Gloria a look. 'Well I've had just about enough of this place. How about you finish off and we'll meet you back in Donut Pizza where it's less noisy?'

'And smelly,' said Dirk, stuffing his notepad back in his pocket.

Marjorie nodded. 'Yeah, I think that's enough work for today,' she said, even though she'd done completely nothing.

The Cool Doods headed out of Smelly Side Supermarket, leaving Rhubarb with Gloria and the Phantom Twizzler.

Rhubarb looked at her two new sidekicks and sighed. If only she could tell Yoshi, Melvin and her dad what she'd worked out.

Suddenly her phone started to ring. She whipped it out of her pocket and slid her finger across the screen.

'Where are you, Rubes?' said Yoshi, staring out of it.

Rhubarb's nostrils waggled. 'Smelly Side Supermarket. Gloria and the Phantom Twizzler are here too.'

'Coowee!' said Gloria, as David Splurg beeped another jar. 'Ooh David, you are a naughty one!'

Rhubarb peered over Yoshi's shoulder. She could see Melvin, looking all grumpy behind him. Her see-through dad was there as well. She could just feel it.

'I think I might've cracked the case, guys,' she said.

'Wait there,' said Yoshi. 'We're just around the corner.'

Ten seconds later, Yoshi ran through the doors of Smelly Side Supermarket. Melvin was behind him, walking all slowly.

Rhubarb looked at the space where her dad was floating, all invisible. Then she glanced at her two new sidekicks, Gloria and the Phantom Twizzler.

'You're safe here, Dad,' she said, and Terry scratched his bum, appearing in a puff of blow off next to Yoshi and Melvin.

Gloria gasped. 'Three for the price of two,' she said. 'Now that's what I call value for money!'

Rhubarb cuddled her dad. 'Sorry if I was a bit grumpy back there.'

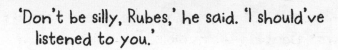

'Don't be silly, Rubes,' he said. 'I should've listened to you.'

Melvin tutted. 'He made us walk the whole way here, just to tell you that.'

Yoshi whipped his notepad out. 'Now what's all this about you cracking the case?'

Rhubarb scratched her dad's bum and started running towards the exit. 'First we've got to get to Donut Zoo!'

Gloria and the Phantom Twizzler waved them goodbye.

BACK TO Donut Zoo

'I can't believe we're here again,' said Melvin. It was fifteen minutes later and he, Yoshi, Rhubarb and Terry were standing outside the entrance to Donut Zoo. 'Can't we just go and arrest Mrs Terrible already?'

Mr Really Nice tapped on the window of his little booth. 'Hello you lot!' He smiled. 'Back so soon?'

Rhubarb nodded. 'Would you mind if we had another look at the reptile house?' she asked.

'Anything for little Rhubarb Plonsky,' he said.
'Here, have a free badge while you're at it.'

The gang zoomed up the path, turned right
at the fat-bummed hippo enclosure, ran
past Longy Long Neck, hung a left at the
giant wooden cut out of a meerkat and
jogged through the tiny bat cave. All apart
from Melvin that is, who was walking.

Crocodile Tony was sweeping up tortoise poo as they skidded to a stop outside the reptile house. 'Not you lot again,' he said.

Melvin strolled up behind them all. 'Come on then,' he said to Rhubarb. 'I suppose you'd better spill the baked beans now that we're here.'

'Yeah, let's hear this theory of yours,' said Yoshi, whipping out his notepad.

Rhubarb took a deep breath. 'Well, it all started when Dad was telling us about Barnaby Toenails.'

Yoshi thought for a second. 'Barnaby Toenails,' he muttered to himself. And then he gasped. 'Hang on a millisecond, that note in your dad's lunchbox - it was signed with a 'T'. Was that for Toenails?'

Rhubarb shook her head. 'At first I thought he might have something to do with it,' she said. 'But then I realised I was looking at the wrong thing.'

Yoshi scribbled in his notepad. 'What do you mean, the wrong thing?'

'It wasn't Barnaby Toenails I should've been thinking about,' said Rhubarb. 'It was my dad's Shrink Ray Gun.'

'The Shrink Ray Gun?' said Yoshi.

Rhubarb carried on. 'Now, I know my dad. He wouldn't have given up on an invention just because the first one didn't work.'

'So you're saying he made another Shrink Ray Gun?' asked Yoshi.

'Not just one,' said Rhubarb. 'I'm guessing he made a whole load of them over the years.'

Terry didn't say anything. He just floated there, silently.

Crocodile Tony, who'd been listening to Rhubarb, shot up his hand. 'So how come I've never seen one of these Shrink Ray Guns in the shops then?' he asked.

Rhubarb shrugged. 'My dad could never get them to work,' she said. 'Until one day, when he had a brainwave.'

'What brainwave?' said Melvin. 'Come on, skip to the end.'

Rhubarb looked at where her dad was floating. 'It was the day my mum and dad took me to the zoo.'

Yoshi flipped back through his notepad. 'When your dad told Crocodile Tony about his Grabby Grabber?'

Mr P thought Crocodile Tony could do with a Grabby Grabber to help him feed the crocs.

(Wouldn't fancy that job if I'm being honest)

((which I am))

'That's right,' said Rhubarb. 'Except you were up to something else as well, weren't you, Dad?'

Crocodile Tony blinked. 'Eh?' he said, looking around. 'Who's she talking to?'

Rhubarb nodded to her dad and he scratched his bum, appearing in a puff of blow off.

'Waaahhh! It's a ghost!' cried Crocodile Tony.

Melvin chuckled. 'Relax, Crocodile Tony. You never seen a ghost before?'

Rhubarb smiled at her dad. 'It wasn't the Grabby Grabber that'd caught your attention that day, was it?' she said, looking up at the plaque on the wall behind Tony.

They all stared at the plaque.

In memory of

Ray the crocodile

'Huh?' said Melvin. 'I don't get it.'

Rhubarb stroked her chin. 'It was the final piece of the puzzle. I realised it when Marjorie and Dirk were talking earlier. Look at the crocodile's name.'

'Ray,' said Melvin, reading it out loud. 'Funny old name for a crocodile.'

'Now think about what my dad was trying to invent,' said Rhubarb.

They all went quiet for a few seconds, then Yoshi clicked his fingers. 'A Shrink RAY Gun!'

Rhubarb nodded. 'That's the brainwave my dad had that day at the zoo,' she said. 'The Grabby Grabber was just a cover.'

'Hang on a millisecond,' said Melvin. 'Are you trying to tell me that this genius idea of Mr P's was that a Shrink Ray Gun would only work on a person who was called RAY?!'

SQUEEZE

RAY

'Or a crocodile,' said Rhubarb. 'That's why he set up the meeting with Crocodile Tony. So he could get inside the cage and try out his invention.'

Crocodile Tony's eyes opened wide. 'So that's why I didn't find a Grabby Grabber in the cage that day,' he said. 'Because he didn't bring one with him.'

Rhubarb shrugged. 'Or he just forgot it,' she said. 'When you didn't turn up, my dad saw his chance and climbed into the cage. I'm guessing old Ray the crocodile snaffled him up before he even got to try out the Shrink Ray Gun.'

Yoshi was still scribbling in his notepad. He stopped and looked up. 'What about that note in the lunchbox, the one signed 'T'?'

'T for Terry,' said Rhubarb. 'It was for my mum, to meet him down here. Dad wanted to show off his invention, but he must've forgotten to leave the note for her.'

'This is making me look very forgetful,' said Terry.

'Yeah come on Rubes,' said Melvin. 'You expect us to believe all this?'

215

Yoshi put his hand up. 'Let's just say it's all true,' he said. 'Why didn't Crocodile Tony find a Shrink Ray Gun in the cage?'

'Yeah, and how did Mr P end up inside the lunchbox?' asked Melvin.

Rhubarb shrugged. 'Yeah, I've still got to work those bits out.'

Melvin sniffed the air, which stank of tortoise poo. 'Well I'm still not smelling it,' he said. 'I say we go down Donut Pottery right now and see what Mrs Terrible's got to say for herself.'

Rhubarb looked at Terry. 'What do you reckon, Dad? Have I rung any bells?'

He smiled down at his daughter. 'I always knew you were clever,' he said. And then he stopped smiling. 'But I'm afraid Melvin's right. It just doesn't add up.'

'WHAT?!' said Rhubarb. 'Of course it does!'

Terry shook his head. 'Trust me on this, Rubes. Melvin's story is the one to go with.'

Rhubarb stomped her foot. 'I can't believe it!
Every time I come up with something,
you poo poo it. Well I've had enough.'

She turned round and started walking off.

'Where are you going now?'
called Terry.

'Brenda the Hut, to write up
my story,' said Rhubarb.
'And none of you can
stop me!'

BAT C

Tiny bat cave

Rhubarb was halfway through the very small bat cave when she heard a footstep behind her. Actually, it wasn't exactly a footstep, it was more of a footFLOAT.

'Who's that?' she said, twizzling round.

But nobody was there.

'It's me,' said Terry's voice. He must've scratched his bum and gone invisible again. 'We need to talk.'

Rhubarb shook her head. 'I've had enough of talking.' She turned back round. 'It's time for me to start writing. Otherwise I'll never win the Newshound Award.'

Terry sighed. 'I know this award means a lot to you, Rubes,' he said, putting his hand on her shoulder. 'But some things are more important.'

'What, like keeping Melvin happy?' Rhubarb starting to walk off again. 'You can't really think Mrs Terrible fed you to the crocodile... do you?'

Terry scratched his bum and reappeared.

It was hard to see him properly in the darkness of the bat cave. He was just a see-through silhouette.

'Of course I don't,' he said. 'That's the whole reason I went along with Melvin's idea.'

'Eh?' said Rhubarb. Now she was really confused.

Terry pulled Yoshi's ghost book out of his pocket and opened it at a folded-over page. 'Nobody knows why ghosts exist,' he said, reading out loud. 'Some believe they are here to complete unfinished business.'

'That's what Yoshi read out yesterday,' said Rhubarb. Why did she feel like he was about to tell her something she didn't want to hear?

'But he didn't finish the sentence,' said Terry.

He looked down at the book again. 'Once a ghost completes their business, they can move on to the next level,' he read.

A bat flew through the air above their heads and Rhubarb screamed.

'The next level?' she said, once she'd calmed down. 'What, like in a video game or something?'

Terry shook his head. 'If you solve this mystery, I could disappear forever.'

Rhubarb whipped her rucksack off her back and pulling out her dad's lunchbox. 'So your unfinished business is solving the mystery of how you ended up inside this thing?'

Terry nodded.

Just then, two more silhouettes appeared inside the bat cave. 'There you are,' said Yoshi's voice.

'We're on our way to Donut Pottery,' said Melvin.

Rhubarb looked at her dad. If it was between the Newshound Award and Terry Plonsky, there was no competition. 'I'm coming with you,' she said.

Melvin peered at Rhubarb in the darkness. 'What were you two talking about?'

'Father and daughter stuff,' said Rhubarb, holding up the lunchbox, about to put it back into her rucksack. Suddenly a bat swooped past her head again. 'Waahhh!' she cried, waggling her arms, and the lunchbox flew into the air.

The lunchbox landed on the floor with a thud. 'Oh great,' said Rhubarb. 'Now it's covered in bat poo.'

Melvin bent down to pick it up. 'Oh dear,' he said. 'Looks like one of the panels is broken.'

He stared into the little compartment behind it and started screaming.

Attack of the haunted lunchbox

Melvin was screaming because a chubby, see-through man was sticking his head out of the compartment in the lunchbox.

'Ooh, my back!' said the man, squeezing the rest of his body out and floating into the air. 'Boy, am I glad to get out of there.'

Yoshi backed against the cave wall. 'Th-that's exactly what Mr P said when he popped out!'

'Who is this guy, anyway?' said Rhubarb.

'Another g-g-ghost!' wailed Melvin.

Terry Plonsky stared at the floating
man. 'Barnaby Toenails. Long time no see.'

'BARNABY TOENAILS?!' cried Rhubarb.

Terry clicked his fingers. 'Oh yeah, I just remembered something,' he said. 'Barnaby was there that day as well.'

Melvin stopped screaming. 'Hang on, so Mrs Terrible DIDN'T feed you to the crocodile?

Yoshi was scribbling in his notepad at super-Yoshi-speed. 'Barnaby Toenails did it instead?'

Terry shook his head. 'No, he just followed me to the zoo, that's all.' He looked at his old pal. 'Once a copier, always a copier, I guess.'

Barnaby Toenails looked around. He was carrying what looked like a see-through Shrink Ray Gun. 'What is this, some kind of miniature cave?'

Terry pointed at the gun. 'My Shrink Ray Gun!' he cried.

'It's been ghostified,' said Yoshi.

Rhubarb stroked her chin. 'So that's what happened to it,' she said. 'Barnaby must've grabbed it when the crocodile ate my dad.'

'He ate me too, you know,' said Barnaby. 'There I was, creeping up on my ex-best friend, about to steal his Shrink Ray Gun, when CHOMP! That blooming reptile gobbled us both up in one go.'

Melvin whistled. 'That was one hungry croc.'

'Next thing I know, me and Terry are
floating there like ghosts,' said Barnaby.
'Hey, how did I end up inside that lunchbox,
anyway?'

Rhubarb did
the time out
sign with her
hands.

'We do not
want to
know the
answer to
that one,
thank you
very much.'

Terry was
still staring
at his Shrink
Ray Gun.

'I can't believe
you stole my
invention all
over again,' he said.
'I knew you were a copier, but a thief as well?'

Barnaby Toenails glared at his old friend. 'That's right, Plonsky,' he said. 'And I've been making a few improvements, too.'

'Don't tell me you've got it working,' said Terry.

Barnaby Toenails nodded. 'Except it's not a Shrink Ray Gun any more.' He pointed it at Terry. 'I've turned it into a Shrink PLONSKY Gun!'

The apology

'Run!' cried Rhubarb, grabbing her lunchbox and zooming out of the tiny bat cave with Yoshi, Melvin and Terry behind her.

'You can't run away from me!' boomed Barnaby Toenails, even though they completely were.

'This way!' shouted Rhubarb, turning right at the meerkats.

Barnaby Toenails pointed his Shrink Plonsky Gun at Terry and pressed the button.

A bright yellow laser shot out the end of it and hit the giant wooden meerkat.

Which could've done with a bit of shrinking, now I think about it.

'Missed me, Toenails!' cried Terry.

Next they ran past the giraffes.

Barnaby shot again, this time hitting Longy Long Neck's neck, not shrinking it at all.

They hung a left at the hippo, and you can probably imagine what happened to its extremely fat bum.

That's right, absolutely nothing.

'Quick, down here!' cried Rhubarb, as she darted along the path towards the main entrance.

'Help us, Mr Really Nice!' screamed Yoshi, skidding to a stop next to the little booth. Barnaby Toenails was still zooming after them, his Shrink Plonsky Gun pointing at Terry.

Mr Really Nice took one look through his window and screamed. 'Sorry, we're closed,' he said, pulling down a faded yellow blind.

Just then, The Cool Doods appeared on the other side of the entrance. 'There you are, Plonsky,' said Hector, slurping on a Donut Pizza cup. 'Where's that story of ours? The Newshound competition closes in half an hour, you know.'

Barnaby Toenails stared down at Hector. 'Did you just call her Plonsky?' He swivelled to face Rhubarb. 'So you're Terry's little girl, are you? Well, I guess this'll work on you as well, then.'

He pointed his Shrink Plonsky Gun at Rhubarb.

'Don't you even think about shrinking my daughter!' shrieked Terry.

Hector stared at Barnaby Toenails then at Terry. He dropped his cup and ducked behind Dirk and Marjorie. 'G-G-G-G-GHOSTS!' he screamed.

Rhubarb was staring straight down the barrel of the Shrink Plonsky Gun. 'What is it you want, Toenails?' she shouted.

Barnaby cackled. 'Let's just say me and your dad have got a little bit of unfinished business.'

Rhubarb stroked her chin. 'Unfinished business?' She tried to think what it could be. Barnaby Toenails already had her dad's Shrink Ray Gun. What else did he need?

She looked over at Melvin, who'd kind of
been acting like her version of Barnaby
Toenails for the last couple of days. She
knew he didn't mean to copy her. He just
wanted to be a detective, that was all.

How would Melvin be feeling right now if
she'd chucked him out of the Daily Donut
gang for copying the way she stroked her
chin, or sniffed the air?

The way Barnaby must've felt when Terry
had him thrown out of their science fair all
those years ago, she supposed.

Rhubarb looked up at her dad's ex-best friend.

'Get ready to go fun size!' he boomed, his finger squeezing the trigger on the Shrink Plonsky Gun.

'I've cracked it!' cried Rhubarb, clicking her fingers, even though she was about to be dolls-housed.

Terry floated over to Barnaby and tried to grab the gun, but his see-through hand just wafted through it.

SQUEEZE

'Cracked what?' said Barnaby, his finger pausing, mid-press.

Terry looked at his ex-best friend, then down at Rhubarb. 'Yeah, what've you cracked, Rubes?' he asked.

'Think about it,' said Rhubarb. 'What's the one thing Barnaby Toenails might want you to say to him, Dad?'

Terry scratched his bald, see-through head. 'I've absolutely no idea,' he said.

Barnaby sighed. 'You see?' He tucked the Shrink Plonsky Gun into his pocket and floated down to the ground. 'He's still got no idea how I feel.'

'Neither have I,' said Melvin.
'Can somebody please tell
me what's going on?'

Rhubarb walked over to Barnaby
and sat down on the floor next
to him. 'You didn't really mean
to copy my dad, did you?'

Barnaby shook his head. 'Course I didn't,' he said. 'I just wanted to be like him. Terry Plonsky was my hero.'

Terry blinked. 'I was your hero?' he said. 'Me?'

Barnaby nodded. 'You broke my heart that day at the science fair, Terry,' he said. 'That's why I turned to the Smelly Side.'

Rhubarb's dad floated over to his old next-door neighbour. 'I - I didn't realise,' he said.

Melvin patted him on the shoulder. 'Don't beat yourself up about it, Mr P,' he said. 'How could you have known?'

'I'm sorry, old pal,' said Terry. 'Really I am.'

Barnaby Toenails looked up at Terry Plonsky and smiled.

'I declare Barnaby Toenails's business officially finished,' said Rhubarb, taking a step back and getting ready to watch him move on to the next level.

Everyone stood there in silence for a second or two, until it all started to feel a little bit awkward.

'Hmm, maybe that wasn't my unfinished business after all,' said Barnaby, pulling the Shrink Plonsky Gun out of his pocket and zapping Terry right on the nose with it.

One last piece of unfinished business

'Ooh, I hate you, Barnaby Toenails!' cried Terry, his whole body going wobbly for a millisecond, then shrinking to the size of a can of Donut Soda.

'Love you too, Terry Plonsky!' cackled Barnaby, starting to fizzle all over, then disappearing with a pop, along with the Shrink Plonsky Gun.

Melvin stared at Rhubarb's dad, floating next to his ghostified snacks, then glanced over at the gap where Barnaby Toenails had just been.

'Did he just scratch his bum?' he asked. 'Because I didn't see him scratch his bum.'

Rhubarb shook her head. 'No, he moved on to the next level,' she said, smiling at her dad. 'Hey, you're pretty cute like that!'

Hector reappeared from behind Dirk and Marjorie. 'Next level?' he said. 'What, like in a video game or something? Ooh, this story is going to be so good!'

Dirk nodded. 'Yeah, we're definitely going to win the Newshound Award!'

Yoshi stopped staring at mini Terry and twizzled his head round to face The Cool Doods. 'What are you lot talking about?'

'THIS,' said Marjorie, snatching his notepad out of his hand.

'Hey, give that back!' cried Yoshi.

Hector chuckled. 'I'm afraid not, Fujikawa,' he said. 'We'll be needing your notes to finish our story.'

'WHAT?' cried Yoshi. 'But they're ours!'

'You copiers!' shouted Melvin. 'Rhubarb, aren't you gonna stop them?'

Rhubarb shrugged. 'Let them have it,' she said. 'We didn't even solve the mystery, anyway.'

Terry floated over to his daughter, looking quite happy to be the size of a can.

'Yeah, we'll never know how Barnaby and me ended up inside my Self-Packing Lunchbox,' he squeaked in his brand-new voice. 'And that's completely fine with me.'

Dirk's eyes turned into slits. 'Hang on a second,' he said, grabbing the notepad off Marjorie and flipping through Yoshi's notes. 'Self-Packing Lunchbox . . .'

'What are you thinking, Measles?' asked Hector.

Rhubarb did the time out sign with her hands. 'Whatever it is, we don't want to know.'

'Why not?' asked Hector. 'Come on, Measles, spill the beans.'

Dirk stroked his chin, then sniffed the air.
'Well, if it's a Self-Packing Lunchbox, maybe
it packed the ghosts of Mr Plonsky and
Barnaby Toenails into itself?'

Hector patted him on the head.
'You've cracked it, Measles!'

'OH, NO,
NO, NO!'

cried Rhubarb.

'Come on,' said Marjorie, running off
in the direction of Donut Pizza. 'Let's
go write it up!'

Rhubarb cupped her dad in her hands.
'They finished your business!' she cried.

Terry stared up at his daughter.
'Well I guess that's that, then,'
he squeaked.

'What's what?' said
Melvin. 'Can somebody
please tell me what is going on?!'

A tear ran down Rhubarb's cheek. 'But you can't go, Dad,' she cried. 'I only just got you back.'

Terry hugged one of her fingers.
'I'm so proud of you, Rubes,' he
squeaked. 'Tell your mum I love her.'

Rhubarb leaned over and kissed him
on his little bald head. 'I love you,
Dad,' she said. Then she closed her
hands around him.

When she opened them again,
he'd gone.

One last bum scratch

'I'm so sorry, Rubes,' said Yoshi, putting his arm round her. Melvin hugged her too.

'This is all getting a bit mushy for my liking,' squeaked a tiny voice, and the three of them looked up.

The sound of a very small hand itching an ever-so-slightly larger bottom broke the silence.

Then Terry Plonsky reappeared.

'Huh,' he squeaked, peering down at his can-sized body. 'Maybe all that lunchbox stuff wasn't my unfinished business after all.'

Rhubarb wiped the tears from her eyes and laughed.

She grabbed her floating dad and gave him a great big smackeroo.

259

'Maybe your unfinished business is this,' she said, pointing at herself, then at him. 'Me and you, I mean.'

Terry thought for a second, then nodded. 'Yeah,' he said, starting to smile. 'Maybe you're right.'

'And the best thing about that,' said Rhubarb, 'is it's not going to be finished for a long, long time!'

Three days later...

It was three days later, like it says above, and the Daily Donut gang were sitting in Brenda the Hut. Suddenly there was a tiny knock on the door.

'Only me,' said mini Terry, floating in.

'Long time no see, Mr P,' said Melvin. 'Where have you been?'

Terry grabbed the see-through packet of crisps floating next to him and ripped them open, which wasn't easy to do, seeing as they were the same size as him.

'With my darling wife Thelma, of course,' he said, chomping on a giant crisp. 'We had a little bit of unfinished business.'

Yoshi chuckled. 'So you decided to let her see you, after all?' he said.

Terry nodded.

'Dad thought he might move on to the next level if Mum saw him,' she explained. 'But we don't need to worry about that any more.'

Melvin smiled at Terry. 'Guess what, Mr P.'

'What?' said Terry.

Yoshi held up a familiar-looking lump of dried-up clay. 'We won!'

'The Newshound Award?' said Terry. 'That's amazing! But why are you holding one of Mrs Terrible's pottery crocodiles?'

'It's not a crocodile,' said Melvin.

Rhubarb chuckled. 'Turns out, Mrs Terrible was making a trophy for the Newshound Award,' she said.

Melvin nodded. 'She just wasn't any good at doing dogs,' he said. 'Didn't I tell you all along it wasn't her!'

Terry laughed. 'Well that explains everything,' he said. 'Congratulations, gang. I always knew The Mystery Of How I Ended Up Inside That Lunchbox would be a winner.'

'Oh, we didn't enter that story,' said Rhubarb. 'The Cool Doods did.'

Terry scrunched his see-through face up. 'Huh?' he said.

'We couldn't enter it as well,' said Melvin. 'We'd've looked like right copiers!'

Yoshi smiled. 'Yeah, we went with something
else instead.'

Terry thought for a second, then he gasped.
'You cracked The Mysterious Case Of The
Squidgy Pavements?'

Yoshi nodded. 'I worked it out when we were
in Donut Pet Cemetery,' he said. 'I figured if
Terry Plonsky could be a ghost, then why
not all those little animals as well . . .'

Melvin sniggled. 'Seems we've been treading
on see-through gerbils this whole time.'

'Well, not exactly,' said Rhubarb. 'Just their see-through poos.'

Terry scratched his little bald head. 'Hmmm, I think I might be getting an idea, guys.'

'What, for another invention?' asked Melvin.

Terry nodded.

'How does...

THE SPOOKY "POOPY" SCOOPER™

sound?'

'Absolutely ridonkulous,' said Rhubarb. 'I love it!'

They all laughed, then they all stopped
laughing, because you can't laugh forever,
can you?

Then Yoshi sighed.

'What's up, Yosh?' asked Rhubarb.

'My notepad. The Cool Doods'll never give it back.'

Rhubarb clicked her fingers.
'Ooh, I almost forgot.'

She pulled a Smelly Side Supermarket carrier bag out of her rucksack.

'We got you these – courtesy of Gloria.'

'For me?' said Yoshi, stuffing his hand into the bag and pulling out a brand new notepad, three new pencils, a shiny new pen and a snazzy plastic pencil case to put them all in.

'For you,' said Rhubarb, patting the notepad. She looked round at the gang and waggled her nostrils. 'Now all we need is another mystery to fill it with!'

Don't start crying, your favourite detectives will be back in...

"My pencil" "case" is a "time machine"

A SUPER WEIRD! ™ MYSTERY

Read my other books - or don't!

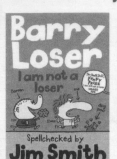

Spellchecked by **Jim Smith**

Commas put in by **Jim Smith**

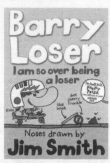

Noses drawn by **Jim Smith**

Pages numbered by **Jim Smith**

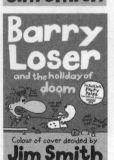

Colour of cover decided by **Jim Smith**

Produced and directed by **Jim Smith**

Absolutely nothing to do with **Jim Smith**

From the squidgy pink brain o **Jim Smith**

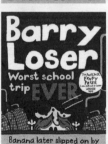

Banana later slipped on by **Jim Smith**

Half-time oranges chopped by **Jim Smith**

Thing on cover always happens to **Jim Smith**

Written by robots controlled **Jim Smith**

Jim Smith

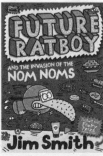

Jim Smith

Jim Smith

Jim Smith